SASSY SISTERHOOD

SASSY & SIXTY

BERNICE BLOOM

DEAR READERS

Dear Readers,

Welcome back to the world of our fabulous sixty-somethings!

As this new chapter opens, Rosie, Emma, Maria, and Lisa have taken the plunge and moved into a magnificent Victorian home together in Esher.

As you step through these pages, you'll join our magnificent foursome enjoying their time together. But life, as we all know, has a way of throwing unexpected challenges into even the most carefully arranged plans. Our heroines will face everything from unwelcome visits from exes to health scares, from the neighbourhood gossips to their own buried secrets. Through it all, they'll demonstrate what we already know—that sixty isn't the end of adventure but a new beginning.

You'll laugh at Emma's outrageous antics, marvel at Maria's ability to organise chaos, warm to Rosie's steadfast loyalty, and perhaps shed a tear at Lisa's hidden courage. You'll witness friendships deepening affection, new dreams emerging, and the past being put properly in its place.

So pour yourself a glass of something delicious (our ladies

would insist), find a comfortable spot, and prepare to be welcomed into the home and hearts of four women who refuse to go quietly—or conventionally—into their sixties and seventies.

The door is open, the wine is breathing, and your favourite sixty-somethings are waiting inside.

Welcome home.

With warmest wishes,

Bernice

P.S. Gerard and Barbara from across the street will likely be watching disapprovingly from behind their curtains as you enter. Pay them no mind – they're both batty as hell.

PREVIOUSLY IN SASSY & SIXTY...

A quick reminder of what happened in BOOK ONE...

Rosie Brown thought life at sixty-three meant gardening, babysitting, and the odd quiet cuppa. Then she agreed to walk her daughter's dog and found herself flat on her face in the park — literally — tangled up in a lead and her own self-doubt. That stumble led to a leap: into new friendships, bold fashion choices, and unexpected joy.

At the heart of it all was the formation of the **Sensational Sixties Squad** — a fabulous fivesome of fierce, funny, and occasionally floppy women:

- **Emma**, the rebellious, party-loving gal with a cigarette in one hand and a cheeky quip in the other.
- **Lisa**, all sleek hair and sharp tongue, a former political journalist with secrets under her smile.
- **Julie**, the paint-splattered artist rediscovering her voice post-separation.
- **Maria**, the shy, sweet late bloomer finding her strength one deep breath (and yoga mishap) at a time.
- And of course, **Rosie**, our heroine, who swapped beige

PREVIOUSLY IN SASSY & SIXTY...

cardigans for leopard print blouses and rediscovered the woman she used to be — and the one she's becoming.

Together, they've survived disastrous yoga, emotional reckonings, ex-husbands, impossible coffee orders, and impromptu nights out. Rosie's decided not to get back with Derek (despite his puppy-dog eyes and unexpected solo walks with Elvis), and the women have vowed to embrace life head-on — one wine-fuelled adventure at a time.

As this book opens, they are all moving into their new house together...

SIXTY, SASSY, AND STARTING OVER

"For the love of God, Emma, be careful. If you drop that, Lisa will come and shoot us all in the face at point blank range," shouted Rosie, watching her friend clutching a boldly decorated ceramic plate while teetering precariously on a stepladder in the entrance hall of their new home.

"Relax," Emma replied, carefully placing the artwork on a high shelf. "I may be 60, but I have the balance of a gymnast. Just watch me as I somersault off here…"

"Nooooo…" Rosie dropped her head into her hands. "No gymnastics, love. I've seen you in yoga. You almost broke your ankle doing tree pose."

"Good point." Emma, hopped down from the ladder with surprising agility. "What's the big drama about that thing, anyway? It's just a plate."

"Just a plate? Not to Lisa, it isn't. It's a Grayson Perry exclusive. Her favourite artist. And it probably cost more than your car."

"There's no doubt about that. In fact, I think the step ladder is probably worth more than my car. Most of Lisa's blouses are worth more than my car. Have you seen what I drive around in?"

"I have, yes. Your car is an abomination, let's be honest. And Lisa does wear remarkably good blouses. But that doesn't change the fact that the art is worth thousands."

Emma looked up at the plate in its new position on a top shelf. "Well, it's safe up there," she said, as she pulled a chocolate bar from her pocket and began unwrapping it, dropping little pieces of foil on the floor without noticing. "You know, I don't think I get art at all. I mean–what's so special about that artwork? It's a mystery to me."

Maria wandered out from the kitchen to join her two new housemates. Her perfectly combed hair held back with two practical clips, sleeves rolled up to reveal forearms slightly damp from scrubbing. Maria had a handsome, plain face, and a neat, capable presence. Not beautiful, but the kind of woman you instinctively trusted to know where the plasters were.

"The previous owners left the place in a shocking state," she said, pulling a travel-sized bottle of hand sanitiser from her pocket and methodically cleaning her palms. "I found dust in places dust has no business being."

"Well, at least we won't catch any exotic diseases with your around," Emma said, crumpling up the rest of her chocolate bar wrapper and tossing it in the general direction of the wastepaper basket. It missed by several inches.

Maria's eye twitched visibly as she watched the wrapper fall. Without comment, she crossed the room, picked it up, and deposited it properly in the bin.

"By the way, which of you left muddy footprints in the hallway? I've just mopped it."

Rosie sighed and held up her hands in surrender, revealing dirt under her fingernails. "Sorry. I think that was me. I couldn't resist doing a bit of weeding in the garden. The previous owners let it get into a terrible state."

"OK, you're forgiven. Come on, I'll stick the kettle on."

Rosie and Emma followed Maria into the kitchen, and had just sat at the large wooden dining room table when they heard a commotion back in the hallway.

There was a clatter of stilettos, a rattle of keys and a string of expletives, as Lisa stumbled through the door, dropped half her bags on the floor, and flopped down next to them.

Glamorous and olive-skinned, Lisa was strikingly beautiful, with a sleek dark bob and cheekbones sharp enough to slice bread. Even mid-collapse, she looked like she belonged on a magazine cover.

"That was quite an entrance. Welcome to your new home," said Rosie, walking out from the huge sunlit kitchen to greet her new housemate. "What the hell are you doing down there?"

Lisa lay prostrate on the oak floor, laughing hysterically. "Actually, it's quite comfortable. I might stay here."

"Get up, you daft mare. You're going to ruin your outfit." Rosie leaned over to help her friend to her feet. Lisa wore a beautiful green velvet coat and rather elegant, fitted trousers with sky-high stiletto boots that had presumably tripped her up.

"Those shoes aren't the best for moving house," said Rosie, noticing how unsteady her friend seemed. "We'll have to get you some trainers before you break your ankles."

"I don't think it's the boots," Lisa said, pressing a hand to her forehead. "I could run a marathon in these. I keep collapsing and seeing double. I think it's the bloody menopause."

It was nothing to do with the menopause Lisa knew that... she'd been through it years ago. Something was wrong, but she couldn't face going to see the doctor. In her experience, no one over the age of 60 ever got out of the doctors' surgery without having to face a barrage of tests, scans and internal rummaging around. Today was supposed to be joyful–the beginning of their adventure together in this beautiful house. Thoughts of illness had no role to play today.

Rosie looked through at the designer bags lying across the steps. They were filled to the brim with clothes. "Good God, woman, you have more designer carrier bags than Harvey Nicholls."

"Almost," said Lisa, steadying herself against the wall. "I think they might have a few more, but it's a close-run thing. Though I'm clearly doing my best to put their children through university."

"Well, I'm very envious. Your wardrobe is stunning."

"You couldn't give me a hand, could you?"

"Of course. Are these bags all you've got?"

"Are you joking?" said Lisa.

"Oh, have you got some in your car?"

"No, I haven't got a car anymore. I sold it, remember? All my stuff is in that..." Lisa pointed to a huge removal van on the street outside.

"Whaaat? I thought we decided to move in temporarily and see how we go... I've just brought essentials."

"Me, too. I only have absolute essentials with me," said Lisa, though her attempt at hauteur was somewhat undermined by how heavily she was leaning against the wall. "This van doesn't represent half of the clothes I've got."

"Come on then. I'll amass the troops and we'll get it all inside."

While Rosie called Emma and Maria to come and help, Lisa sat down on the step and took a moment to admire their beautiful new home. It was a very grand house with six bedrooms and lots of land, just on the outskirts of Esher. The Victorian windows caught the autumn sunlight, making the place glow warmly.

The whole process of moving in with friends reminded Lisa of arriving at her university digs back in the 80s - fresh-faced, wearing a ra-ra skirt, an Adam and the Ants t-shirt and more sparkly blue eyeshadow than the two women in Abba combined. An outfit that would now require its own historical preservation order.

She remembered the excitement, and the prospect of fun, jollity and adventures.

There would probably be less nightclubbing this time round since all her new housemates were in their 60s, and the place would be considerably cleaner, but she knew that there would be parties, gentlemen callers and enough alcohol to sink a small ship.

The sound of footsteps shook her out of her daydream, and Emma and Maria appeared next to her, beaming from ear-to-ear.

"Lisa. How are you doing, lovely? Fab coat, by the way," said Emma. Tall and sturdily built, with a strong, pretty face and cropped hair that always looked as though it had been styled mid-sprint, Emma never wore makeup and dressed like she'd just come from walking a large dog across muddy fields.

"Thank you," said Lisa, trying to suppress another wave of dizziness.

Maria ran up to Lisa next and helped her to her feet. "Have you lost weight? You're even more skinny than usual."

"I don't think so," said Lisa. "I am a bit off my food, but nothing much."

Another lie, she thought. I've lost nearly a stone in two months. Can't keep anything down some days.

"We'll look after you, and feed you up," said Maria, her practical nature already asserting itself.

"We can certainly do that," said Emma. "We need to get a massive takeaway down you. You look pale."

"I'm fine. Honestly, I'm just 60, menopausal and tired."

"Oh, well - join the club. Menopause or not, we are going to have so much fun! I can't believe we're here," said Maria, jumping up and down like a schoolgirl.

"This nutcase was here at about 6 am , cleaning everything," said Emma, putting her arm around Maria. "She was on her hands and knees, scrubbing the kitchen floor when I arrived."

"It was filthy," said Maria. "You know how I can't bear dirt of any kind. If I could vacuum the vacuum cleaner, I would."

"Oh, lord. This has the potential for disaster. I should tell you right at the start that I'm not very tidy," said Rosie, smiling apologetically at Maria. Sweet-faced and soft around the edges, Rosie had the sort of warm smile that made strangers feel like friends. She wasn't a stunner like Lisa, but she looked damn good for her age and still turned heads when she wanted to.

"I'm not tidy, either," said Emma. "Robert used to go nuts about it when we were married. We'll be messy together."

"Or we'll get a cleaner," said Maria, unable to face the thought of messy housemates.

"Oh My God. Don't mention cleaners," said Emma. "I have a checkered history with domestic help."

"What do you mean?"

"Did you tell about the time I employed a secret cleaner?"

"No," said Rosie, as the women stepped outside and headed towards the huge van. A man in blue overalls was unloading things... pictures, furniture, mirrors, and shoes. Mainly clothes and shoes, to be fair. Less a wardrobe, more a small department store on wheels.

"Give me 10 minutes to organise all these, then we can start carrying them in," said the guy.

The women went and sat on the small wall at the front of the house to wait, Rosie keeping a careful eye on Lisa who seemed unsteady even sitting down.

"OK, Emma - we want to hear about the imaginary cleaner."

"No, she wasn't imaginary. She was quite real. She was a secret. It was a while ago, when the kids were little. I decided I wanted to go down to part time at work, and Rob said that if I wanted to cut back my hours, then we had to let the cleaner go."

The women all gasped.

"Do your own cleaning? What is he? Some sort of monster?" said Rosie.

"Well, yes. Pretty much. Anyway, I got rid of Simona - the cleaner - like he said, and my life was a complete misery. I hated it, and ended up shoving things I hadn't washed into the wardrobes where they'd fester along with all the unironed clothes."

"Yuk." Maria gave a little shake to show how appalled she was at this conduct.

"I knew life couldn't go on like this, so I rang Simona and asked her whether she could come back. I told her that, under no circumstances, should she tell anyone that she was working for me again, and that I would pay her in cash rather than bank transfer. Also - she had to come after my husband left for work. I wasn't having an affair; I was having a cleaner. Somehow, that felt more forbidden."

"Oh, so she really was a secret cleaner?" said Maria.

"I'm not proud of myself, but needs must, and all that," said Emma. "Anyway, this system worked really well. She'd come and clean two mornings a week and Rob was none-the-wiser. It was magnificent. I'd lie on the bed reading, or I'd watch TV while Simona cleaned the house from top to bottom, and Rob would come home and comment on how tidy it all was."

"Well, that's truly magnificent," said Rosie. "The perfect crime."

"Indeed, it was. Then one morning, Rob came home from work halfway through the morning because he'd forgotten his phone. I ran upstairs, grabbed Simona and threw her into the wardrobe, then leaned against it. Like a normal person would. My husband came in and asked whether I'd seen his phone anywhere.

"'No, love, I haven't,' I said, keeping all my weight against the wardrobe door.

"'Can you help me look for it?' he said, but I knew I couldn't leave my position against the wardrobe, or the door would swing open and Simona would tumble out. She was a large woman - way too big for the wardrobe that I'd pushed her into. I knew that if I moved, I'd be rumbled.

"My mind went through all the scenarios if she fell out. I realised I'd have to say we'd been having an affair... Rob would be far less bothered about that than he would have been if he'd found out about my secret cleaner."

"So, what happened?" asked Maria. "Did you get away with it?"

"Just about. Rob found his phone and left. As soon as I heard the front door close, I let Simona out of the wardrobe. She stumbled onto the carpet, looking confused and distressed.

"I no longer work. Is no good," she said, wearily, before taking her box of cleaning implements and heading for the door. I never saw her again."

"Oh My God. You are nuts," said Lisa. "I've never heard of anything so ridiculous."

"Oh blimey - I've got loads of stories like that. I'll tell you about my imaginary job later."

"Imaginary job?"

"Oh yes," said Rosie, as the van driver walked towards them. "This nutcase here used to buy suits and smart shoes for a job she didn't have..."

"OK, ladies. If you could help by taking some of these clothes in, that would be great. Carry nothing heavy, I'll handle them."

As they climbed the grand staircase with bags of luggage, Rosie smiled to herself. A six-bedroom house had been hard to find, but it was worth the search. This place was perfect.

Lisa had claimed the largest room on the second floor, with Emma taking the equally lovely room next door. The first floor housed Maria's cosy space and two guest rooms, while Rosie had fallen in love with the converted attic at the top of the house, with its exposed beams and views across the garden.

She'd expected it to be bigger than it was, given the width of the house. Her room seemed only to take up half the attic. But it was lovely. She was thrilled with her hideaway at the top of the house.

Lisa paused halfway up, pressing a hand against the wall to steady herself. "Just catching my breath," she said, attempting to wave off the others' concerned looks. "These stairs are rather steep, aren't they?"

Don't let them see how bad it is, she thought fiercely. Not yet. Let us have this day, at least.

It took four women and one man several hours to bring up all of Lisa's belongings. Her room had a lovely en suite, and a large dressing room, but it still didn't look as if it would be big enough to house everything she'd brought. Luckily, there were two spare rooms on the second floor next to Maria.

"It might be best if we leave these toiletries here," said Rosie, indicating the two cardboard boxes full of lotions and potions. "There's no room on the bathroom shelves for them."

"Yes, of course. Just leave them there and I'll go through them later. I'll need to decide which anti-aging serums to keep and which to donate to the Natural History Museum."

Rosie left the room to see how many more bags and boxes there were to unpack. She paused on the landing to check her phone again. Still no response from Mike, the guy she'd been seeing for the past few months. She'd left him three messages this week, but he seemed to avoid her calls. She pushed away the nagging worry and focused on helping Lisa settle in.

There was a collection of distressed late century French furniture, a large gilt-edge mirror and many, many cases of clothes sitting outside her friend's room, ready to be organised.

"What's in this one?" asked Rosie, unzipping a cream case and seeing an exquisite blue silk blouse inside. In truth, she was quite enjoying all this nosing around in Lisa's bags. There were so many luxurious clothes - it was lovely to see them all.

"Are these all silk? Wow - they're so elegant, Lisa."

Beneath the sky-blue silk, there were a dozen sophisticated blouses and shirts in every colour you could imagine; dark green, coral and a soft cream colour caught Rosie's eye.

"Lisa - where shall I put these?"

Despite her obvious exhaustion, Lisa directed operations from her perch on the bed. "Just leave them by the dressing room, that goes under the bed, the painting needs to go higher," she called out, before closing her eyes against another wave of dizziness. Even half-conscious, her artistic direction was impeccable.

Rosie looked at Lisa - her beautiful bronzed skin looked waxen, her breathing shallow. Rosie lay the duvet over her and left her to sleep. There was plenty of time for unpacking. They could do that tomorrow.

She closed the door, left the room, and walked down the elegant, wide stairway. She felt like she was in an episode of Dynasty... the sunlit entrance hall below and the vast kitchen leading into the garden at the back of the house. All that was missing was Joan Collins and some oversized shoulder pads.

Rosie could hear gentle chatter coming from the kitchen as Maria and Emma unpacked and tidied up.

How lovely it was to have people around. It seemed like only yesterday she had been sitting alone at home, nursing her wounds after Derek left her. Then she had bumped into Emma and Lisa when dog-walking in the park, and soon after that Maria had arrived, tears streaming down her face at the discovery that her husband, David, was having an affair.

Four women, each bearing the scars of life's disappointments, finding new joy and purpose in a massive house together. The Golden Girls, but with better real estate and more expensive wine.

She was sure they would get on each other's nerves from time to time, and there were bound to be minor disagreements, but what joy to be in a lovely big house with a group of like-minded women.

As the sun set, casting a warm glow over the chaos of moving day, the four women gathered in the kitchen. Despite her earlier exhaustion, Lisa had rallied enough to join them for drinks, though she nursed her wine rather than drinking it with her usual enthusiasm.

"To new beginnings," Rosie said, raising her glass.

"To friendship," added Maria.

"To adventures," Emma chimed in.

Lisa looked around at her new housemates, her eyes sparkling despite her pallor. "To the Sensational Sixties Squad," she declared. "May our lives be as fabulous as my shoe collection. And considerably more stable than my magnificent but treacherous high-heeled boots."

And may this illness please not be as serious as I think it is, she added silently, raising her glass a fraction higher.

THE STREET'S WORST-KEPT SECRETS

"IT'S our first morning as a delightful commune," said Rosie, balancing the last sliver of smoked salmon onto the small nub of bagel that was left, and popping it into her mouth. "I think we should go out and meet the neighbours. You know, like civilised people."

"Really?" said Lisa. "Do we need to? I don't think of myself as a go out and meet the neighbours sort of person. Isn't it only people in daytime American soap operas who do that?"

"Is it?"

"Yes - newcomers arrive and the pesky, nosy neighbours are straight over with a basket of muffins and a cheery smile. I'm not a basket of muffins sort of person. I'm more of a ˆsort of person."

"We don't have to take muffins, we just need to turn up and say hello and learn a little about our neighbours. Don't you think it would be a civilised thing to do?"

"Since when have we made any pretence at being civilised?" said Emma, walking into the kitchen and pinching a slice of avocado off Lisa's plate. "We're heathens. That's why we all get on so well. Our idea of culture is watching foreign films with the subtitles off while drinking boxed wine."

"All I'm suggesting is that we knock on a few doors. It would be good to know whom we live next to," said Rosie.

"I guess," said Lisa. "I'm not sure why we care. Excellent use of 'whom' though. If we don't worry about the terminal preposition, your grammar is the most civilised thing in this kitchen."

"Thanks, I think," said Rosie. "Though I don't know what that terminal thing is. Anyway - we're in a community. We should get to know all the people around us, so we feel part of something. Also, for security."

"I kind of agree with Lisa," said Emma. "We've got our own little community here...we don't need anyone else."

"OK...let's put it this way; there might be some incredibly handsome men living just down the road. Imagine if we never attempted to go out and meet them?"

Lisa and Emma looked at one another. "Good point, well made," said Lisa, as Emma reached over to steal another slice of avocado. Lisa pulled the plate away quickly. '

"Come on, then - let's go. There's no point staying here if Lisa will not let me steal her food."

Half an hour later, the women were assembled and ready to go. Rosie in an emerald blouse and smart jeans, Emma in a t-shirt and cargo pants that had seen better days, Maria in a blouse and skirt, and Lisa, who had insisted on dressing for the occasion, in a flowing maxi dress and oversized sun hat.

"Now remember, ladies," said Rosie, looking back at the women as if they were a line of little ducklings, "we want to make a good impression. We're not just four single women living together; we're respectable members of the community."

As they rounded the corner onto Maple Street, the women encountered their first neighbour - a distinguished-looking gentleman pruning his rose bushes. Not quite the handsome hunk they'd hoped to meet, but he seemed harmless enough.

BERNICE BLOOM

"Good morning! I'm Rosie, and these are my friends. We've just moved into number 42 Lavender Lane. It's lovely to meet you!"

The man straightened, eyeing the group with a mixture of curiosity and amusement. "Ah, yes. The new... arrivals. They were all talking about you. I'm Gerald Fitch. Welcome to the neighbourhood."

"I'm thrilled to hear we're being talked about," said Lisa, stepping forward and turning on the charm. "Gerald, darling, those roses are simply divine."

She deployed the word "darling" like a tactical weapon. Gerald looked flustered by the glamorous woman's attention.

"Goodness. Thank you. Here you go," he said, cutting off a rose, removing the thorns and handing it to her. Lisa blew him a kiss and Gerald's face turned scarlet. His complexion now perfectly matching the rose he'd just surrendered.

"There are four of you, are there? Living in the house?"

"Gerald, Gerald..." came a voice from the lovely cottage behind him. "What on earth are you doing?"

"Hide it," he said to Lisa, as a well-upholstered woman came into view. "Quickly hide the rose."

Lisa held the rose behind her back, while Emma lifted her hand to her face to hide her sniggering. Gerald's panic suggested his wife kept him on a leash shorter than the pruned stems in his garden.

The woman had short grey hair, with a side parting and a fringe which flickered across her forehead. It was very unflattering, though certainly not the worst thing about her appearance. Her expression suggested she'd been sucking lemons while doing her tax return.

"These are the ladies who have just moved into the big house up the road," he said as the woman approached. "They came to introduce themselves."

"I've heard all about you," said the woman whom they assumed to be Mrs Fitch.

"I hope some of it was good," said Rosie.

"No, not really. I'm going to be honest with you - we all miss the lovely couple who used to live in there. They moved away and rented it out. I'm surprised you took it."

"What an adorable woman you are," said Lisa, bringing the rose to her nose and smelling it extravagantly to provoke her.

"Are you? But it's a beautiful house. There were lots of people wanting to rent it," said Rosie.

"Were there? Even given the history."

"What history?" asked Emma, suddenly intrigued.

"It's haunted. There's a creepy dark-haired man who haunts it, looking for his lover who died of food poisoning. Some say the poisoning was on purpose. I don't like to gossip, but that's what they say."

The women stood and stared, unsure what response such a revelation demanded.

"Murdered," said the woman.

"Oh God. Such nonsense. I'm afraid I don't believe in ghosts," said Lisa. "But it's lovely to meet you all the same. Thank you for the rose, Gerald."

Gerald went scarlet again, as his wife stared at him. "Sorry, Barbara," he said.

"OK - let's go," said Rosie, pulling Lisa away. "Lovely to meet you, Gerald and Barbara."

Once they were out of earshot, Rosie turned to Lisa. "We're here to befriend the neighbours, not terrify them. There's a difference between making an impression and declaring war. Why didn't you keep the rose hidden?"

"Sorry - she just annoyed me."

"Honestly, love. Rise above it. What's that thing you're always saying? When they go low; you go high."

"Yeah, you're absolutely right. I don't feel myself at the moment. I promise to behave from now on."

"Thank you."

"Anyway, we have more important things to worry about. Our house is haunted," said Maria. "Did you hear that? It's haunted."

"There's no such thing as haunted - she's just a stupid old cow with too much time on her hands," said Lisa.

"Ummm...what did we just agree?" said Rosie.

"Yes. Sorry again."

"Well, she was a stupid old cow, but there are ghosts. Imagine!" said Maria

Rosie and Emma looked over at Lisa, knowing their friend would have plenty to say on this subject, but Lisa grimaced theatrically and managed not to comment.

"If a ghost haunts your house, it can cause all sorts of problems. Things get moved around and the ghostly form can appear at the end of your bed and stare at you."

"It's weird though, don't you think? I mean, if people defy the biology of death and come back to earth, all they do is move things around and watch people sleeping?" said Lisa. "That's less supernatural phenomenon and more creepy roommate behaviour."

"They probably do lots of other things as well, but moving things around and haunting are the only ones I've heard of."

"Yeah. OK. We might have to agree to disagree on This whole ghost thing."

"If you disagree with me, you're disagreeing with loads of the world's greatest scientists who believe in ghosts."

"Who?" asked Rosie, unable to stop herself from being drawn into the conversation.

"I don't know their names."

"Exactly," said Lisa, laughing to herself.

Maria shook her head. Living with these women was going

to be great, and she loved them all, but Lisa irritated her. The woman thought she was superior to everyone else. She had a good job as a writer and was well-connected, but that didn't make her any better.

Rosie put an arm round Maria and gave her a big squeeze. "You come and get me if the ghost appears. I'll protect you. Anyway - at least it's an interesting place to live. It would be awful to be somewhere boring."

"That's true," said Maria. She could hear Lisa and Emma laughing about the idea of ghosts in the house, and making 'Ooooo...' noises behind her. She ignored them.

"Where are we heading next, then?" she asked Rosie.

"I think we should go to the place that looks like a farmhouse. It's tucked just behind the High Street, so we could grab a coffee at the place on the corner. Sound OK?"

"Sounds great," said Maria, falling into step with Rosie while the other two hung back.

Rosie and Maria arrived at the farmhouse and knocked on the door. There was no answer. They walked to the side of the house, but still no sign of life.

"Come on, let's get a coffee," said Rosie. "At least we tried."

"There's no one in," Maria shouted to Lisa and Emma, who were still a considerable way behind. "Fancy a coffee?"

"It's almost midday," replied Lisa. "Let's treat ourselves to a glass of wine."

There were cheers of agreement and the plans were suddenly changed; they would have drinks and lunch and meet the neighbours another day.

"Come on then, what wine does everyone want - I'm buying," said Lisa. "A bottle of Chablis? Two bottles?"

"We'll be drunk!" said Rosie.

"So what? It's not like we have to operate heavy machinery or make important life decisions today."

"Yeah, go on then...get two. Let me give you some money."

Lisa batted away Rosie's hand clutching a £20 note and walked towards the bar. Rosie watched her go, until her attention was drawn to a man sitting there - silver-haired, distinguished, with kind eyes that crinkled at the corners as he smiled at something the bartender said. The kind of man who appeared in advertisements for luxury watches or exceptionally good whisky.

"Earth to Rosie." Lisa put the drinks down on the table. "See something you like?"

Rosie felt a blush creep up her cheeks. "I was just... admiring the decor."

"Uh-huh," Emma said, a knowing grin spreading across her face. "And would this 'decor' happen to be about six feet tall, silver-haired, and looking mighty fine in that blue shirt?"

Before Rosie could respond, Lisa had already sprung into action. "Leave this to me, darlings. I'll do a little reconnaissance."

Despite Rosie's protests, Lisa sauntered over to the bar, striking up a conversation with the mystery man. From their booth, the others watched with a mixture of amusement and anticipation.

"Ten quid says she comes back with his number," Emma wagered.

"Twenty says she comes back with his entire life story and a dinner invitation," Maria countered. "And possibly his dental records and blood type."

A few minutes later, Lisa returned, a triumphant smile on her face. "Ladies, allow me to tell you all about John Collins. He's a semi-retired physician, volunteers at the local animal shelter, and does some modelling. Oh, and he's single." This last bit of information was delivered with a significant look at Rosie, who felt her blush deepen.

"I'm not interested," she said. "I'm seeing Mike, remember."

"Oh, yes - Mike, who has gone missing."

"I'm sure he'll reappear at some stage."

John approached their table, his smile warm and genuine. "Lisa tells me you ladies are new to the neighbourhood. Welcome to Esher. I hope you're finding everyone friendly."

"No - we're not new to the area. We've all lived here a long time, but we've just all moved into a new house," said Maria.

John nodded slowly and smiled. He had the most fabulous dimples.

As John chatted, Rosie noticed his eyes kept drifting back to her. Or was she imagining it?

By the time he excused himself to leave for a modelling job at a local arts group, Rosie was thoroughly charmed.

"Well," Lisa said as soon as John was out of earshot, "I think we can chalk this up as a very successful first foray into the Esher social scene as housemates. We've got the neighbourhood buzzing, we've learned all about a ghost in the house, and our Rosie's caught the eye of the local hottie. Not bad for a day's work."

"I haven't 'caught' anyone's eye," Rosie protested, though she couldn't help but smile. "Besides, I've just told you - I'm seeing Mike."

"The same Mike who hasn't returned your calls all week?" Lisa asked with a raised eyebrow.

Rosie's smile faltered. "He's probably just busy with work. He's a doctor, you know. Lots of emergencies."

"Too busy to send a text?" Emma asked sceptically. "I don't think so, darling. Trust me, when a man wants to be in touch, he finds a way."

Rosie sighed, reluctantly acknowledging the truth in Emma's words. Mike's silence was becoming increasingly difficult to ignore or explain away.

"Anyway," Maria said, clearly trying to change the subject, "let's not dwell on absent men. What should we do for the rest of the day?"

"I saw a lovely little antique shop on the high street," Lisa suggested. "We could browse there after lunch?"

"Perfect," Rosie agreed, grateful for the distraction. "And I need to pick up some groceries for dinner tonight."

As they settled back with their wine, the conversation moved on, but Rosie couldn't help but notice John at the bar, sending one last smile in her direction before he left.

Perhaps her friends were right. Perhaps Mike's silence was telling her something she needed to hear. And perhaps, just perhaps, their new neighbourhood held more possibilities than she'd initially thought.

DUST, DISCOVERIES AND DISCRETE INQUIRIES

The local library was bubbling with life. So many people striding around, searching for books and busy reading. It was a perfect Tuesday morning. It filled Maria's heart with joy. She had slipped out of the house early, before the others woke, leaving a note about buying some milk in order to make it to the library without detection from her housemates who may mock her enthusiasm.

"Hello, I'm Susan. Can I help you?" The librarian, a woman about Maria's age with steel-grey hair and kind eyes, approached as Maria was scanning the local history section. "You look a bit lost."

"No, don't worry. I thought I'd be the only one here this early."

"Tuesdays are surprisingly popular. Let me know if you need any assistance."

"Actually, you might be able to help. My friends and I have just moved into a house on Lavender Lane and I'm researching its history. I was keen to look at local records, old newspapers, that sort of thing."

The librarian's expression shifted subtly. "Ah. Which house would that be?"

"It's number 42; the large Victorian one, with the garden that stretches back toward the woods."

Susan's eyes widened slightly. "I see. The Blackwood House. That property has quite an interesting history. Being new residents, you'd be keen to find out all you can."

Maria felt her excitement rise. In the local history section, Susan pulled out several leather-bound volumes and a stack of archived newspapers. "I'm afraid none of these have been digitised yet, so it's a case of working through things methodically. Start with these," Susan suggested. "The property records are interesting."

Left alone with the materials, Maria began her research. She spread the documents across table and pulled out a notebook. Her pen moved rapidly across the page as dates and names emerged: The property had been built in 1868–a grand Victorian manor commissioned by Edward Blackwood, a wealthy textile merchant whose fortune had been made in the booming industrial north before he moved south.

Maria traced his family through the property records... Edward, his wife Charlotte, and their three children: Thomas, Elizabeth, and James. The youngest son, James, at twenty-four, captured Maria's attention. His name appeared repeatedly in local newspaper social columns—charity events, hunting parties, musical recitals—often mentioned as "the most eligible bachelor in the county." Yet there was no record of any formal courtship or engagement.

The property records were straightforward enough until 1892, when the house passed to Theodore Richmond. Maria scanned the transaction details, pausing when she found a note: "Property transferred following unfortunate circumstances." The document offered no further explanation.

Maria continued her research through the morning, discovering that there had been a tragedy at the house – the young son James and a kitchen maid had died. They'd been poisoned. This was astonishing. The family had departed hastily. The circumstances were vague in the official records, though local rumours had apparently persisted for decades. Rumours about murder, revenge and suicide then ghostly presences…angry ghosts haunting everyone.

The thought of hearing ghosts in the night made her feel quite terrified. As she contemplated the horrors of things that go bump in the night, a sudden bang made her leap up in the seat. Then another bang. Christ, what was that?

She looked up at the high window next to her and saw Gerald Fitch there, peering through, only half his head showing as he waved vigorously.

"Hello love," he shouted. "You doing alright there?"

Maria stood and waved back, feeling unable to shout anything given that she was in the middle of a library.

"Cat got your tongue," he shouted. "Not saying hello?"

"It's a library," she said.

"What you saying?"

"IT'S A LIBRARY, I CAN'T SHOUT," she shouted back. She sat back down and saw Susan heading towards her, a finger on her lips.

"I'm going to have to ask you to leave if you shout again," she said. "This is a place for quiet reading. We can't have you shouting through the windows to the men."

"I wasn't. I…Oh, it doesn't matter. Yes – I'm sorry, I won't shout again."

She turned her attention to a bundle of newspaper cuttings, as her phone buzzed with a text from Rosie: *Where are you? Have you got lost buying milk? Lisa's not well - could use your help.*

Maria gathered her things together, carefully marking pages with slips of paper and organising her notes.

"I'll be back soon," she promised Susan as she hurriedly

checked out several volumes. "There's so much more to uncover." Her voice couldn't hide her excitement despite her concern for Lisa.

Susan smiled knowingly. "Old houses always have stories worth discovering. Some are happier than others. We just need to make sure we do it quietly."

When Maria arrived back, her flatmates were assembled in the kitchen. Rosie and Emma were on the sofa while Lisa was at the table looking remarkably well, surrounded by stacks of papers and research materials, her fingers flying over her laptop keyboard with energy and enthusiasm.

"Sorry to drag you back, but I was worried," said Rosie, standing up and whispering to Maria. "Now look at her. She was barely conscious about an hour ago. It's like someone flipped a switch. I don't know what on earth is wrong with her?"

"That's... good though, right?" Maria said.

"Yes, fantastic. But she seems to go from really very ill to absolutely fine in minutes. I'm worried."

"Perhaps we need to sit her down and talk to her properly... persuade her to go to the doctors."

"Yes, definitely."

"Come on then, let's talk to her."

"What? Now?"

"Yes, now," said Rosie. "Come on, it's important."

Rosie texted Emma and explained what they were about to do. Once they'd seen her look at her phone, they nodded at her and she joined them as they approached Lisa. The three women positioned themselves strategically around their friend, who was typing furiously on her laptop, fingers flying across the keyboard with surprising energy for someone who'd been practically unconscious an hour earlier.

"Lisa, darling," Emma began, her voice gentle but firm. "We need to have a quick chat."

Lisa looked up from her screen, clearly irritated by the interruption. The smile that appeared on her face seemed forced. "Can it wait? I'm in the middle of a crucial chapter—the politician's heroic handling of the financial crisis. It's all complete rubbish, of course, but the deadline is tomorrow."

"I'm afraid it can't," said Rosie, sitting down beside her. "We're concerned about you."

"About me? Whatever for?" Lisa's laugh was a touch too bright. "I'm perfectly fine and terribly busy."

Maria, ever practical, cut straight to the point. "You were barely conscious an hour ago, and now you're typing like you're possessed. That's not normal, Lisa."

"Oh, that." Lisa waved a dismissive hand. "Just a little dizzy spell. Nothing to worry about. Happens all the time when I'm on a deadline."

"It's not just today," Emma said. "We've all noticed the patterns. Good days followed by bad, extreme fatigue, and then these bursts of energy that seem to come out of nowhere."

Lisa's smile faltered. She glanced at her laptop screen, then closed it slowly. "I'm managing it," she said, her voice lower. "I have a system."

"Managing what exactly?" Rosie pressed gently. "Lisa, we're your friends. Your family now. Whatever it is, we can face it together."

For a moment, Lisa's carefully maintained facade cracked. She looked tired, the lines around her eyes more pronounced. "It's nothing dramatic," she said finally. "Just some... health issues I've been dealing with for a while."

"Have you seen a doctor?" Maria asked.

"Several," Lisa admitted with a sigh. "They all say different things. One says it's chronic fatigue, another suggests fibromyalgia, a third insists it's all in my head." The bitterness in her voice was palpable.

"What are you doing for treatment?" Emma asked, reaching out to take Lisa's hand.

Lisa hesitated. "Well, that's where I may have been a bit... creative. I've been managing it my way. Diet, rest when I absolutely must, and then... pushing through when I can. The writing helps, actually. When I'm in the flow, I don't notice the symptoms as much."

Rosie exchanged concerned glances with Maria and Emma. "That doesn't sound like a sustainable plan, Lisa."

"It's worked for me so far," Lisa insisted, but there was less conviction in her voice.

"We're worried about you," Rosie said simply. "We care about you. And we want you to get help—not just for the symptoms, but to understand what's happening."

Lisa looked at each of them her expression softening. A tear slid down her cheek, which she quickly wiped away. "Well, when you put it like that, how can I possibly refuse?" She straightened her shoulders. "I'll make an appointment with a specialist. A proper one this time."

"And we'll go with you, if you want," offered Emma. "Moral support, second pair of ears, whatever you need."

Lisa nodded, visibly moved. "Thank you. I might take you up on that." She cleared her throat and flipped open her laptop again. "Now, if you don't mind, I really do have a deadline to meet. These memoirs won't ghost themselves."

The three women shared a look of cautious relief. It wasn't everything they'd hoped for, but it was a start.

"Come on," Rosie whispered, gesturing toward the seating area. "Let's give her some peace."

Settling into the comfortable chairs, Rosie poured fresh cups of tea for the three of them, glancing occasionally at Lisa who was now typing furiously, pausing only to press her fingers against her temples.

"Do you think she'll really go to the doctor?" Maria asked in a low voice.

"I hope so," Rosie replied, setting down the teapot. "I'm worried about her. Those headaches seem to get worse."

Emma nodded thoughtfully. "She puts on a brave face, but I've noticed how she struggles some days. One moment she's barely able to keep her eyes open, the next she's working like she's possessed."

"She's written some incredible books, hasn't she?" Maria mused. "She mentioned ghost-writing for all sorts of famous people."

"Must be fascinating work," said Rosie. "Imagine having all those insights into people's lives and careers. Much more interesting than what I did – I was a teacher and then I did PA work and ran a small secretarial and admin business."

"There must have been some fun times as a teacher," said Emma.

"It drove me nuts, to be honest. I loved teaching, but I didn't enjoy acting as a prison warden every day, trying to control 30 wild teenagers."

Emma smiled. "To be fair, Rosie, I bet you were a very good prison warden. I can imagine you making a student cry just by raising your eyebrow—the infamous Eyebrow of Doom that launched a thousand detentions."

Rosie laughed, shaking her head. "You sound just like Mary. My daughter always says I have 'eyebrows of doom.'"

"In defence of teaching, there's nothing quite like the feeling of helping a child understand something for the first time. Seeing that light bulb moment... it's magical."

As Rosie continued chatting about her days in the classroom, the others listened intently. She told them about the challenges of keeping a roomful of school children engaged, the joy of nurturing young minds, and the bittersweet feeling of watching her students grow up and move on.

"Of course, now I get to experience it all over again with my grandchildren," Rosie concluded with a soft smile. "It's different, but just as rewarding."

"Well, I for one am glad I never had to deal with tiny humans," Emma declared. "I think I'd rather deal with a roomful of cutthroat bankers. At least bankers don't smear peanut butter on the conference room walls. Usually."

From across the room, they heard Lisa chuckle faintly without looking up from her screen.

Maria raised an eyebrow at Emma. "I keep forgetting you used to be a high-flying finance type. How on earth did you end up in that world?"

Emma grinned, launching into a tale of her unlikely journey from art school dropout to banking prodigy.

"Picture this," she said, leaning forward. "Me, twenty-one years old, sitting on the floor of my bedsit surrounded by half-finished canvases and a letter saying I'd been kicked out of Central Saint Martins for, and I quote, 'lack of commitment to the artistic process.'" She mimicked quotation marks with her fingers. "What they actually meant was I kept missing critiques because I was working night shifts at that pub in Soho."

Maria settled back into her armchair. Emma's stories were wonderful… but never quick.

"So there I was, crying into a pot of beans on toast, when my flatmate Sylvia bursts in wearing this ridiculous 1980s power suit with shoulder pads out to here," Emma extended her arms. "She takes one look at my miserable state and says, 'For God's sake, Em, stop crying. I need someone to type up these reports by morning, and my usual girl's called in sick. Fifty quid if you do it tonight.'"

Emma reached for her tea, eyes twinkling with the memory. "I'd never used a proper typewriter before, but fifty quid was a week's rent. So I followed her to this massive office in the City. Middle of the night, just me, Sylvia, and the cleaners. She hands me a stack of handwritten notes about interest rates and market projections—completely meaningless to me—and points to a desk in the corner."

"You must have been terrified," Maria interjected.

"Terrified? I was mostly thinking about what I could buy with fifty quid!" Emma laughed. "Anyway, I'm about three pages in when I notice something odd in the analyst's notes. There's this projection about currency markets that doesn't match the conclusion. I'd been dating this Swedish exchange student who'd prattled on endlessly about the krona, so I actually knew something about it."

She paused for dramatic effect. "So I typed a brief note in the margin: 'Calculation error on page 4? Swedish interest rate forecast seems wrong.' I thought nothing of it."

"You didn't," Maria said, smiling at the familiar turn in the story.

"Three days later, Sylvia shows up at our flat again. Says her boss wants to meet the person who caught the error. Next thing I know, I'm sitting across from this terrifying woman in an even bigger power suit who slides a calculator across her desk and starts firing questions at me."

Emma's hands moved animatedly as she continued. "Six months later, I'm enrolled in night classes for accounting while working days as the lowest-ranking analyst at Barrington Phillips. Had to sell all my art supplies to buy my first proper suit."

"But you were good at it," Rosie prompted.

"Turns out I had a head for numbers all along. My art professors always said I was too analytical, too precise. Banking liked those qualities." Emma's voice softened. "The real turning point was the Matthews merger in '90. The team had been working for weeks on this massive corporate takeover. Everyone was looking at spreadsheets and projections, but I noticed something in the company's art collection reports."

"Art collection?" Maria raised an eyebrow.

"The target company had this substantial corporate art collection they'd been depreciating oddly on their books. I'd studied enough art history to know the pieces were massively undervalued. When I pointed it out, my bosses realised the company was worth thirty percent more than they'd calculated." Emma shrugged. "I know their assessors would have discovered it, but they were impressed that I had. They made me part of the core team after that."

"And the rest is history," Maria concluded.

"A decade of balancing books instead of painting them," Emma said with a wistful smile. "Then I met Robert, got pregnant, and that was that."

The room fell quiet for a moment, broken only by the soft tapping of Lisa's keyboard across the room.

"Would you change it?" Rosie asked. "If you could go back?"

Emma considered this, her fingers absently tracing the pattern on her mug. "No," she said finally. "I wouldn't. Art never left me—it just transformed. I spent 10 years finding patterns in numbers instead of colours. Plus, without that banking career, I wouldn't have met Robert, and much as our relationship is well and truly over, I'm glad I had the kids."

As the room softened into silence, Maria spoke up. "I think I'd like to have a job, you know—do something with my life which has purpose. Am I too old, though? I mean, who would ever employ me?"

"Darling, it's never too late to start. Why, just look at us! We're all embarking on fresh adventures at our age. Who says you can't do the same?" said Emma.

"Remember how you helped me reorganise my closet last week? You have a real eye for design and organisation. Why not look into interior design courses? You could start small, maybe help friends and neighbours, and see where it takes you," said Rosie.

"Do you really think I could?"

"Of course you could," Rosie assured her. "And with your organisational skills, you'd be a natural. Why, I bet you could turn this entire house into a showcase of beauty and efficiency."

"Let's not get carried away," Emma teased. "Some tasks are beyond even Maria's considerable talents."

As they continued to brainstorm ideas for Maria's potential new career, they were startled by Lisa suddenly exclaiming, "You have got to be kidding me!"

They turned to see her answering her phone with a grimace. She mouthed "sorry" to them before slipping into what they now recognised as her "ghostwriter persona," her voice taking on a deferential tone that was completely at odds with her usual confident demeanour.

"Yes, of course, sir. Your heroic stance on that bill was indeed a turning point in modern politics. Oh, absolutely, I'll emphasise your pivotal role in... what's that? The environmental protection act? Of course, how could I forget your passionate advocacy for... I'm sorry, did you say you opposed it? Ah, I see. How clever of you, sir."

The three women exchanged glances, trying to stifle their laughter. Emma was particularly enthralled, miming increasingly dramatic gestures to match Lisa's verbal gymnastics.

Finally, Lisa ended the call, letting out a long-suffering sigh and running her hands through her hair in frustration. She looked over at her housemates and rolled her eyes dramatically.

"Everything alright?" Rosie called over.

"Just peachy," Lisa replied with heavy sarcasm. "Apparently I need to rewrite an entire chapter because our esteemed leader has suddenly remembered he was on the opposite side of an issue than what he told me last week. The cognitive dissonance is staggering."

"Politicians," Emma said with a dismissive wave. "The only profession where contradicting yourself is considered a skill."

Lisa laughed and turned back to her work with renewed determination, while the three women on the sofas returned to talking.

"I'll feel so much better about everything when she has seen a doctor," said Rosie. "Let's keep nagging her until she makes an appointment."

THE PROSTITUTE AND THE DIRTY VIDEO

Maria woke suddenly, heart thumping against her ribs. There were noises. Unmistakable sounds—a pitter-patter and scampering sound coming from downstairs. She heard tiny footsteps. Definitely not the familiar tread of anyone who lived in the house.

She pulled the duvet up to her chin. There really were ghosts. Now she'd heard them, she knew for sure. Maria lay back, ears straining in the darkness.

"Anyone here?"

Maria bolted upright, clutching her chest.

Oh my God.

That was definitely not one of her housemates. The tone was all wrong. It had to be a ghost. Possibly one of those creepy Victorian children from horror films. Perhaps it was carrying its head under its arm

She fumbled for her dressing gown, brain racing through contradictory plans: Should she investigate, or barricade the door with furniture? But then would ghosts respect physical barriers? Surely they'd just float through walls, rendering her bedroom fortress useless.

With trembling fingers, she cracked open her door and whispered into the darkness. "Are you a ghost?"

The childish giggles stopped suddenly.

"Are you a ghost?" she repeated, this time a breathy, wavering whisper straight out of a low-budget séance.

"I mean no harm," she continued in her newly adopted spectral sing-song. "Please identify yourself, spirit. Or perhaps provide an otherworldly sign of your intentions..."

"What on earth are you doing?" came a voice behind her. Maria whirled around, hand clutched to her thundering heart, to find Rosie walking down from her attic room in her pyjamas.

"Did you come down because of the ghosts?" Maria asked.

"Ghosts? What are you talking about? And since when do you talk like a Victorian medium?"

"I thought I heard ghosts. Downstairs. The ghostly presence of children. Be careful."

"I think we'll be OK," said Rosie. "It's just Mary and the kids. I gave her the spare key and told her she could drop them off."

"Oh, right. OK. Well, great. That's good, then. I'll get dressed."

Rosie smiled to herself as she walked down to greet her daughter. Maria was so keen for there to be a ghost in the house that she'd taken leave of her senses.

"Hello, love, how are you?" she said, giving her daughter a big hug.

Mary looked exhausted. "I'm so sorry to drop in like this, but I'm at my wit's end. Daisy and George haven't slept through the night in weeks, and I have so much work to do. This head of marketing role is much bigger than I thought it would be. Could you watch them for a few hours while I do some work?"

Rosie's heart went out to her daughter. She remembered all too well the challenges of raising young children. "Of course, sweetheart. Why don't you head off?"

"Yaaaayyy!" shouted the children, jumping up and down, knowing how spoiled they'd be in grandma's hands.

"Would it be OK if you dropped them at a birthday party at 3pm? It's only round the corner, then Ted will pick them up from there. I've written the address on here, and their party clothes and the birthday present are on the table over there."

"No problem at all, love."

"Can I just have a word first, Mum," she said hesitantly, "I've been meaning to tell you something. Dad's been asking about you."

Rosie stiffened. "Derek? What does he want?"

"He says he misses you," Mary replied. "He and that Pauline woman split up months ago, and he's been talking about how he made the biggest mistake of his life."

"Has he indeed?" Rosie said, her voice carefully neutral.

"He's asked if he can come see you," Mary continued. "I told him I'd ask you first."

"Tell him..." she began, then paused. "Tell him I'm happy, Mary. Truly happy. And that chapter of my life is closed."

Mary studied her mother's face. "Are you sure?"

"Yes, love. He really hurt me when he had the affair, then we managed to become friends for a while. He even met Mike, remember? But then Emma bumped into him, back with Pauline. I just don't want anything to do with it all...it's too painful."

"He's a dick," shouted Emma, coming down the stairs and hearing the conversation. "Sorry – I know he's your dad, but he can't bounce from one woman to another and back again."

Rosie smiled. "We're very protective of one another," she said to her daughter.

"No, I understand. I told him I'd say something that's all," said Mary, opening the door to leave and walking straight into two strapping young men standing on the doorstep. "Good heavens," she said. "Please tell me you haven't come to see my mum. I don't think I could cope with that."

The taller of the two smiled. "Hi, I'm Josh, and this is my brother Joe. We're Emma's sons. Is she around?"

Emma's jaw dropped. "Josh? Joe? What on earth are you doing here?"

As the young men were ushered inside, the house descended into cheerful chaos. The twins, excited by the new arrivals, began running circles around everyone's legs while Josh and Joe chased them.

Maria took on the role of chef, whipping up healthy snacks that somehow managed to be both nutritious and appealing to toddler palates.

Emma, meanwhile, was caught between managing the twins and catching up with her sons. "So," she said, bouncing a giggling toddler on her knee, "what brings you boys to our neck of the woods?"

Josh and Joe exchanged glances. "Well," Josh began, "we were worried about you, Mum. When you told us you were moving in with a bunch of strangers, we thought..."

"You thought I'd lost my marbles," Emma finished for him, chuckling. "Well, as you can see, I'm doing just fine. More than fine, actually."

"I can see that. This place looks like fun."

Eventually, the lure of watching a football match pulled Josh and Joe away – off to meet friends in the pub, so Daisy and George ran back over to their grandma.

"You want to watch a film," said Rosie, as she and her two little grandchildren sat on the sofa, waving goodbye to the boys.

"I want to watch Ty Annick," said Daisy, her tiny face scrunched with determination.

"Ty Annick?" Rosie queried.

"Yes. Ty Annick," repeated Daisy.

"Come on, love, get a grip," said Emma. "They're clearly saying Titanic."

"Yes!" squealed both children.

"OK," said Rosie, mentally calculating how much psychological damage a sinking ship movie could inflict on five-year-olds.

"Shall I put it on?" asked Emma.

"Do you think this is appropriate, though?"

"I don't know, but they must have seen it before, or they wouldn't know the name," said Emma, finding the film and hitting play.

The two little children on the sofa squirmed with excitement as the film started. The same could not be said of Rosie…within minutes she had dropped off to sleep.

"Wake up, wake up. What's that? What's that? What do they mean?"

Rosie woke up to see Daisy, pointing at the screen with jam-sticky fingers that Rosie couldn't remember her having when the film started.

Rosie blinked rapidly and looked at the screen, desperately trying to figure out what catastrophic scene her grandchildren were now absorbing.

"What's a prostitute?" Daisy asked, her voice carrying innocent curiosity. "They said it was a prostitute."

On the screen, there was a woman on crutches. Rosie's mind went completely blank.

"Oh, a prostitute is a woman who has crutches," Rosie heard herself say. "You see those wooden sticks that that lady is using to walk with?"

"Yes?" chorused the children.

"Well, they're called crutches, and prostitute is the name of someone who uses them."

"Oh," said Daisy. George looked very confused.

"You're going to regret saying that at some point," said

Emma, wearing the smug expression of someone who didn't have grandchildren to lie to yet.

"What was I supposed to say?" asked Rosie, glancing at her watch. Her life had become a series of ticking time bombs planted by innocent questions.

"We don't want to watch this anymore," said Daisy, her attention span dissolving as quickly as it had formed. "The boat is too boring."

"Okay, let's switch it off." Rosie was relieved she didn't need to answer any more questions about prostitutes. "It's time for us to go to your friend's house to play now anyway."

"I don't want to go yet. I want to watch the film about the dirty car," said George, his bottom lip jutting out in a pout so practised it could win awards. "The one where they wash it and then it goes vrooooom-fly-fly." He accompanied this with sound effects and arm movements that narrowly missed knocking over Rosie's cherished Royal Doulton figurine.

"Which film about a dirty car?" Rosie asked, mentally scrolling through Netflix's children's section and drawing a complete blank. Perhaps it was one of those bizarre YouTube videos where people power-washed vehicles to inspirational music?

"You know, the one we watch with Granddad Derek, about a dirty car, and they clean it all," George insisted, with the exasperation of someone explaining basic concepts to an alien. "It goes in the water and doesn't sink like the boring boat."

Daisy nodded vigorously. "And the lady doesn't want the children because they're too noisy and messy, like when you call Mummy and say we're too noisy and messy."

Rosie made a mental note to stop having phone conversations within earshot of her grandchildren.

"Chit chit bang, bang," said George.

"Ah, Chitty Chitty Bang Bang, the film about the dirty car that they clean and mend and fly through the sky."

"Yes," said George.

"Let's watch the dirty car film when we get back, shall we?" said Rosie. "We need to get ourselves ready now to go to Jessica's party."

Rosie dressed the children in their finest clothes, even squeezing George out of his Superman outfit—a battle that involved negotiations worthy of international diplomacy and promises of ice cream. She finally strapped them into the car and off they went.

"Remember," she said, adjusting the rearview mirror to catch their angelic faces. "We're going to be polite today and not hit anyone."

"And George mustn't shout 'bottoms,'" added Daisy helpfully, referencing last week's disaster at the library.

"That's right."

"Bottoms, bottoms, bottoms, wee and poo," shouted George.

Rosie's knuckles whitened on the steering wheel. This was going to be fine. Totally fine.

She lifted them out of their seats and walked them to the front door of a house that screamed "we have a dedicated crafting room and colour-code our spice rack." In they ran without so much as a backward glance, squealing when they saw their friends and squealing even harder at the sight of a big, red bouncy castle in the garden.

"Come in, come in," said Felicity, a mother so glamorous at 3 pm on a Saturday that Rosie felt like she'd shown up to a royal wedding in her gardening clothes. Felicity's daughter, a miniature diplomat in patent leather shoes, stood beside her.

"Rosie! Darling!" Felicity air-kissed somewhere in the vicinity of Rosie's left ear. "Did you bring snacks? Oh, you didn't. Never mind."

Rosie remembered these parties so well. She was astonished that so many parents had stayed. When Mary was young, the parties would either be MS (Must Stay) or the most popular ones—DAR (Dump And Run)—where you'd get to drop the children off and have an afternoon to yourself. This party was very much in the MS category.

It seemed that all the mothers had stayed here, forming their usual battle formations. Tracy, clipboard in hand like a weapon of mass organisation, was already delegating party tasks to parents. Sophie arrived fifteen minutes late, looking bewildered by the concept of a doorbell, her gift hastily wrapped in what appeared to be last Sunday's newspaper.

Carmella was inspecting the buffet table with the intensity of a bomb disposal expert, presumably searching for dairy, gluten, or joy to remove before her precious offspring came galloping up and ate the 'wrong' thing.

The main topic of conversation was around what new school the children might go to in September. Mary had told Rosie that Kervin Primary School was the most popular one. It had the best reputation locally, and mothers would jump over the moon to get their children in there. Many had started to go to church where they knew the head teacher sang in the choir, and others were giving generously to the charitable foundations associated with the school.

After a couple of hours, Ted turned up to pick up the children. She watched how Daisy and George ran over to him when they saw him, grabbing a leg each and squeezing tightly.

"Are you ready to go home?" he asked.

"No, we can't go home yet," said Daisy, wrapping herself around Ted's leg like an enthusiastic koala. "We want to go home and watch Granny's dirty video. Can we go and watch the dirty video?" Her voice had that special piercing quality that children reserve exclusively for public spaces.

George jumped up and down, his voice joining in perfect synchronisation. "The dirty video! The really REALLY dirty one!"

Everyone spun and looked at Rosie. The room went quiet

except for the distant sound of a bouncy castle pump and what might have been Rosie's reputation deflating simultaneously. She looked up in alarm, her face progressing through shades of red previously unknown to science.

"I don't know what they mean," she croaked.

"Yes, you do! The dirty video. You said we could watch your dirty video."

"Yes," added Daisy. "You said, you promised we're going to sing along to the dirty video."

"Oh, no—not dirty film! You mean the dirty car film, the one about Chitty Chitty Bang Bang."

There were lots of vacant faces all around her.

"No dirty videos. Don't worry about any dirty films," she said. "They don't mean that at all. They mean Chitty Chitty Bang Bang. They call it the dirty car film. I don't know why they're calling it a dirty film. I would never show them a dirty film, would I, Ted?"

She watched Ted leave the room, his shoulders shaking as he laughed to himself.

"Ted, Ted, don't walk away! I was just saying I wouldn't let them watch a dirty video."

"No, and nor should you after what the police said," Ted replied, making the matter about 100 times worse.

While Rosie had been trying to explain, other mothers had started to arrive. Daisy looked up as Molly's mum walked in.

"Look, it's a prostitute!" Daisy shouted on seeing Molly's mother on crutches, her voice cutting through the party chatter like a foghorn. The room fell so silent you could hear the bouncy castle deflating in the garden. "My granny said you were a prostitute."

Felicity's perfectly pencilled eyebrows shot up so high they nearly disappeared into her hairline. Tracy's clipboard clattered to the floor. Carmella's hand flew protectively over her child's ears as if the word itself might infect him.

"No, no, I didn't say that," said Rosie, her face burning hotter than the candles on the birthday cake. "No, no, of course not."

"Yes, you did! Yes, you did!" Daisy insisted with the unwavering conviction only a child could muster. She pointed an accusatory finger at Molly's mother. "You said Molly's mummy is a prostitute. That's a prostitute."

Rosie dropped her head into her hands then looked up at Ted's quizzical face. "We were watching Titanic," she tried to explain. "Daisy asked me what a prostitute was, and there was someone on the screen on crutches. I just said a prostitute was someone on crutches. I was struggling, Ted. I didn't know what to say."

"It's okay, everyone. Don't worry," said Ted. "I'll take her away now. She needs to go back to the home. I think her medications are wearing off."

"No, no, no," said Rosie, desperately trying to explain why she had been encouraging her children to watch dirty videos and calling other mums prostitutes. Her hands flapped about like distressed birds, knocking over a cup of organic apple juice that spread across the table.

Carmella looked like she might need smelling salts.

"She'll be okay once we get her back to the nursing home," Ted continued, his eyes twinkling with mischief. "She just needs a straitjacket, that's all. They lock her up at night, but she's mostly harmless."

SKELETONS IN LAVENDER LANE

*I*t was a peaceful morning. Rosie was tending to her herb garden, still reeling from a day looking after her grandchildren and alarming all the local mothers. Lisa was engrossed in her ghost-writing project, and Emma was attempting to master the art of French toast.

With her housemates all busy, it was time for Maria to make a sift exit and return to the library. She was determined to learn more about the mysterious deaths and subsequent sale of the house.

The library's silence enveloped her as she pushed through the heavy oak doors. The familiar scent of aged paper and furniture polish greeted her—a perfume more comforting to Maria than any designer fragrance.

"I thought you might be back," Susan said, appearing with a cart of materials. "I pulled some additional records for you. Town council minutes, parish records, some personal journals that were donated to our archives years ago."

"Thank you," Maria said, genuinely touched by the librarian's thoughtfulness.

Susan pushed her tortoiseshell glasses higher on her nose. "I think it might be worth you looking through this first...it is very interesting."

Susan handed over a yellow file stuffed with sheets of paper. "These are notes from a young girl called Alice Henderson. She lived in the house during the 1920s."

"Yes, I remember seeing that family name in the property records."

"Alice kept journals about her time there. This was hers." Susan placed a leather-bound volume on the table. "It was found in the attic by owners in the 1950s and donated to us. I've never shown it to anyone before, but you live there now. Perhaps you have a right to know."

Maria carefully opened the journal, its pages brittle with age.

"I'll leave you too it. Please don't start shouting out to your boyfriend outside this time. There were lots of complaints after you left."

"He wasn't my boyfriend," Maria said, but Susan had gone.

The leather binding creaked in protest. Alice's handwriting was neat and precise, the ink faded to a sepia brown that made Maria squint in the diffused library light. She began reading entries.

January 8, 1923 – Father says I am imagining things again. Mother suggests I need more fresh air. But I know what I saw. A man standing at the foot of my bed last night. Dark hair, pale skin, the saddest eyes I've ever seen. When I screamed, he vanished. Like smoke. Father searched the house but found nothing. He thinks I had a nightmare.

January 12, 1923 – He came again. This time he spoke. He called me Eliza. When I told him that wasn't my name, he seemed confused, then angry. The temperature in my room dropped so quickly I could see my breath. I'm writing this under my covers with our new torch. I dare not sleep.

January 20, 1923 – I've found newspaper clippings in the library about James Blackwood and Eliza Winters. They died here, in this house, in 1892. Food poisoning, the papers said. But the man – the ghost – told me otherwise. "He poisoned us both when he found out," he whispered. "My father couldn't bear the scandal of his son loving a servant." I asked who he was. "James," he said. "I'm waiting for her. She promised she'd come back to me."

Maria felt a chill run through her as she read, goosebumps rising on her arms despite the warmth of the library. Her heartbeat quickened, a cold sweat breaking out along her hairline. This confirmed her suspicions. Her hand drifted to her throat, suddenly dry. But why would the father kill his son? It made some sort of sick sense that he might be tempted to poison the pregnant woman, but did he need to poison his son instead? The entries continued:

February 3, 1923 – Mother is ill. Dr. Bennett says it's anaemia. She's so pale, so tired all the time. Father wants to send her to the seaside to recover. I told him it's not anaemia. It's this house. It's James. He's draining her somehow. I can feel it too – a constant tiredness. As if something were pulling at my very essence. Father refuses to listen.

Maria stopped. Could that be why Lisa was ill? Was the house draining her?

February 17, 1923 – I found a photograph today in the attic. A portrait of the Blackwood family. James looks exactly like the man in my room. But there was something else – the kitchen maid standing in the background. When I looked closely, I gasped. She could be my twin. Same hair, same eyes. No wonder he calls me Eliza. Father caught me with the photograph and became angry. He burned it in the fireplace. Said I was becoming obsessed. But I saw his fear.

The next few entries documented Alice's mother growing weaker, while Alice herself experienced strange dreams in which she was Eliza, living her life, falling in love with James, plotting to run away together. She wrote of "memories that aren't mine" and "feelings for a dead man."

The final entry sent shivers down Maria's spine:

March 10, 1923 – James came to me again last night. He touched my face. His hand passed through me, but I felt it – cold like winter frost. "You're not her," he said. "But you could be. Let me in. Let me in and we can wait for her together." I knew then what he wanted. Part of me wanted to say yes. To end this exhaustion, this constant draining feeling. To understand these foreign memories that plague me. But I am Alice Henderson, not Eliza Winters. I told him no. He became enraged. The mirror shattered. My brushes flew across the room. I'm writing this as Father packs our things. We're leaving today. I pray we're not too late. I pray he doesn't follow.

Maria turned the page, but it was the last entry. Her hands trembled slightly, leaving a faint fingerprint on the aged paper. She looked up at Susan, who had been watching her read.

"What happened to Alice?" Maria asked, her voice barely above a whisper.

Susan sighed, her weathered hands folding together. "She recovered, eventually. Married, had children. Lived into her eighties. But she never spoke about what happened in that house. Her family donated her journal after her death. Said she'd kept it locked away her entire life."

Maria nodded, turning back to the other materials. Council records showed multiple complaints about the house over the decades – unusual noises, strange lights, one particularly strongly-worded letter from a tenant in 1935 demanding the town investigate "the malevolent presence" in the house. All complaints were noted, filed, and apparently ignored.

Parish records revealed more: Theodore Richmond, the bachelor who'd purchased the house from the Blackwoods, had become increasingly reclusive during his time there. The vicar had noted concerns about his mental state in several entries. The final mention of Richmond came in April 1906:

"Called to Lavender Lane upon report of strange odours. Found T. Richmond deceased in master bedroom. Coroner ruled natural causes, though the state of the body and room suggest otherwise. House to be thoroughly cleaned before sale.

Richmond often spoke of 'James' in his final months, though no person of that name was known to visit. May God have mercy on his troubled soul."

Maria's research continued through church records, finding a surprise: Eliza Winters had been buried in the parish cemetery, but James Blackwood's body had been transported north to the family plot in Northumberland.

"They separated them," Maria murmured, a knot forming in her stomach. "Even in death."

Then she noticed something...Blackwood's body was buried two weeks before Eliza's. Why would that be? Why would they have kept Eliza's body for so long before burying it?

Maria stood up, pushing back her chair with a scrape that echoed through the quiet library. Her legs felt stiff after sitting so long. She went to find Susan, who was cataloguing records in a nearby alcove, the soft tap of her keyboard a rhythmic counterpoint to the library's stillness.

"These burial records," Maria said, pointing to the dates, her finger pressing so hard on the paper that it nearly tore, "they show James was buried almost immediately, but Eliza wasn't interred until two weeks later. That seems... unusual."

Susan examined the documents, her brow furrowing. "You're right. That is strange, especially for that time period. Bodies weren't typically kept that long before burial."

"Could there be an explanation? Perhaps her family couldn't afford a proper burial right away?"

Susan shook her head, her silver bob catching the light. "Even for servants, the household would generally handle funeral arrangements promptly. Let me see if we have anything else that might explain this."

She disappeared into the archives, the sound of her sensible shoes fading into the distance. Maria checked her phone—a text from Rosie asking if she was OK. Guilt pricked at her, but she couldn't leave now. Not when she was so close to the truth.

Susan returned minutes later with a thin folder, slightly out of breath. "Medical examiner's notes," she explained.

Maria opened the folder with careful fingers, the paper cool to the touch. The handwriting was faded but legible, the clinical observations of death recorded in detached, professional script. She scanned the pages, her eyes widening as she reached the report on Eliza Winters.

"Oh my God," she whispered, her heart suddenly pounding in her ears.

"What is it?" Susan asked, leaning closer, the scent of her lavender perfume momentarily competing with the musty books.

"The dates," Maria pointed to the top of each report, her hand now visibly shaking. "James died on March 17, 1892. But Eliza... according to this, she didn't die until March 30th. Almost two weeks later."

Susan's eyes widened behind her glasses. "But the newspaper reported they died together. Food poisoning at the same meal."

Maria's mind raced as she continued reading, a flush of excitement spreading across her cheeks. The medical examiner had noted "traces of arsenic consistent with ingestion" in James's body. But Eliza's report was different: "Cause of death: laudanum overdose. Self-administered."

"She wasn't killed by the poisoned wine," Maria said, her voice barely above a whisper. Her mouth had gone completely dry. "She survived it."

Susan reached for another archival box, pulling out a small leather-bound volume. "This might help. It's the diary of Mary Carlton, the Blackwoods' housekeeper at the time."

Maria carefully opened the fragile diary, scanning until she found entries from March 1892, the scent of old leather and decay filling her nostrils:

March 17 - Tragedy has struck our house. Master James took ill suddenly at dinner, collapsing before our eyes. The kitchen maid Eliza was also stricken, though not as severely. Master Edward forbade us from calling the doctor until it was too late for the young master. The poor boy died within hours. Eliza remains unconscious but breathing. Master Edward insists she be moved to the carriage house, away from the main residence. I fear what this might mean.

March 18 - Master James is to be buried tomorrow. The official story is that both he and the girl died of mushroom poisoning. But Eliza still lives, though barely. I have been tending to her in secret, against Master Edward's wishes. Mrs. Blackwood brings medicines when she can, though her husband watches her closely. The girl drifts in and out of consciousness, calling for James.

March 20 - Eliza woke properly today. When I told her James was gone, buried two days past, she wept as though her heart would break. Through her tears, she revealed that she carries James's child. They had planned to elope, to marry in Scotland beyond the reach of Master Edward's disapproval. She begged me to help her recover, to escape north as they had planned, to raise the child that would be James's legacy.

March 29 - I returned from my half-day to find Eliza missing from the carriage house. I searched in panic, finally finding her in the attic room where she and James would meet in secret. She had somehow dragged herself there, despite her weakened state. The small table was set as if for a celebration, with two glasses of wine. One had been drained. She lay beside it, clutching a letter to her chest, already cold to the touch. The letter was addressed to James, speaking of joining him soon. She had taken all of Mrs. Blackwood's laudanum. I could not bear to move her from that place where she had been happiest with her love. I will tell the others in the morning, but tonight, I keep vigil.

Maria couldn't speak for a moment, overwhelmed by the tragic story unfolding before her. Her eyes burned with unexpected tears. The weight of this long-ago tragedy pressed on her chest, making it difficult to breathe. Just like their neighbour Angela had said—food poisoning, possibly deliberate. The local gossip had preserved elements of truth across the decades, like insects trapped in amber.

"It wasn't a double murder," she finally said, her voice cracking. "Edward Blackwood meant to kill them both with the poisoned wine, but Eliza survived. When she learned James was dead..."

"She took her own life to join him," Susan finished softly, her usual professional detachment slipping. "Just like Romeo and Juliet."

Maria flipped forward in the housekeeper's diary, finding the final entry about Eliza, her pulse quickening with each turn of the brittle page:

March 31 - Eliza was buried today, the official story being that she finally succumbed to the same poisoning that took Master James. Only myself, Mrs. Blackwood, and God know the truth. Master Edward insisted on separate burials - James in the family plot up north, Eliza here in the parish cemetery, as far from each other as possible. But I know their souls have found each other, beyond his reach at last. Mrs. Blackwood slipped Eliza's locket into her coffin - the one with the miniature portrait of James that he had given her. "So she won't be alone," she whispered to me at the graveside. I pray they find peace together in the hereafter that was denied them in life.

"So that's why his ghost might still be here," Maria whispered, a lump forming in her throat. "He died not knowing what happened to Eliza. He's still searching for her, not realising she chose to follow him."

Susan gave her a measured look, adjusting her glasses. "It's certainly a tragic story. Many local historians believe these unresolved tragedies leave a... lingering impression on properties."

Maria gathered the documents, her hands trembling slightly with the weight of this revelation. "I need copies of these. All of them."

As Susan went to make copies, the mechanical hum of the

machine breaking the library's silence, Maria sat back, contemplating the tragic tale...her mind raced with possibilities. Not just murder, but star-crossed lovers separated by death itself. James, poisoned by his father for loving a servant. Eliza, surviving only long enough to realise her love was lost, then choosing to join James rather than live without him.

And now, their spirits remained separated still - James haunting Lavender Lane, searching for the woman who had promised to meet him in the afterlife but whom he somehow couldn't find.

The story was more complex, more heartbreaking than she'd imagined. Maria pictured the sealed attic room, untouched for over a century. What might still be there? The wine glasses? The letter Eliza had written to James? Some tangible connection that might help his restless spirit find peace?

"I've pulled additional materials for you," Susan said quietly, returning with a stack of photocopies and leading Maria to a secluded reading room, their footsteps echoing on the parquet floor. "These weren't in the general archives." She placed the documents on the table. "Personal papers from Theodore Richmond, the man who bought the house from the Blackwoods. They were donated anonymously in the 1950s with instructions not to catalogue them with the family records. The kind of specifications that practically screamed 'nothing suspicious here, move along' in bureaucratic whispers."

Maria's heart quickened as she opened the portfolio, the leather cool beneath her fingers. Inside were journals, correspondence, and what appeared to be research notes, all written in a cramped, meticulous hand.

"He became quite obsessed with the Blackwood tragedy," Susan explained, tapping a fingernail against one particularly dense page of notes. "According to these papers, he purchased the house specifically to investigate what really happened to James and Eliza."

The journals revealed a man consumed by the mystery. Early entries showed genuine scholarly interest, but as Maria read on, Theodore's writing became increasingly frenzied, even paranoid.

One entry caught her eye: "I am certain now that James visits this house. Last night, the temperature dropped so suddenly that my breath clouded before me. He is searching, always searching. I have tried to tell him about the girl's fate, but he does not seem to hear me."

Digging deeper, she discovered correspondence between Theodore and several mediums and spiritualists popular during the late Victorian era. They discussed "making contact" and "bridging the divide between worlds." Most striking was Theodore's detailed documentation of his own declining health during his time in the house.

"Energy completely depleted again today," one entry read. "Dr. Morris suggests a tonic for my nerves, but he does not understand. It is James. He draws from me, searching, always searching."

"Theodore's obsession eventually consumed him," Susan said quietly, her voice dropping to a near-whisper despite the empty library. "He spent his final years in that house, rarely venturing out, documenting what he believed were James's attempts to find Eliza."

As Rosie prepared to leave, Susan pressed one final document into her hands, her touch lingering a moment longer than necessary. "Property records from 1892," she explained. "Theodore Richmond made some renovations after purchasing the house. Note the changes to the attic."

Maria scanned the document, her eyes widening. According to the records, Richmond had sealed off a portion of the attic – creating a hidden room accessible only through a concealed panel in the master bedroom closet. Her pulse accelerated. The sealed room must still be there, waiting all these years, perhaps containing the answers they needed.

"Why would he do that?" Maria wondered aloud, her mind already picturing the hunt for the hidden entrance, what treasures or horrors might lie beyond.

Susan's expression was grim. "Because rumours are that Eliza poisoned herself there. Whatever the truth, no one has opened that room in over a century."

Maria nodded slowly, tucking the document into her bag, the paper crinkling against her notebook. A hidden room. A ghost searching for his lost love. A house that drained life from its residents. And now, four sixty-something women who had unwittingly stepped into the middle of a century-old tragedy.

Maria was deep into her research when her phone buzzed in her pocket. She fished it out, surprised to see Emma's name lighting up the screen.

Come back soon. The gardeners have arrived and it's MAGNIFICENT viewing...

A photo appeared seconds later. Maria nearly dropped her phone on the desk.

Two young men were captured mid-work in the garden: tanned, impossibly fit, and—thank the heavens—shirtless. One was kneeling by the flower beds, muscles rippling as he yanked out weeds. The other was stretching toward a high branch, creating an abdominal topography that belonged in a anatomy textbook labelled "Perfection."

Maria glanced around furtively, suddenly conscious that she was a 62-year-old woman ogling a photo of men young enough to be her sons.

More pictures please, Maria typed back quickly, abandoning all pretence of dignity.

They're even better in the flesh. If I were you, I'd get yourself home. ASAP.

Maria checked her watch. She'd planned to spend another

hour researching, but some opportunities in life simply couldn't be missed. She could practically hear Lisa's voice in her head: "Darling, history is forever. Sweaty young men with garden implements are fleeting treasures."

She hurriedly gathered her things together and headed toward checkout, nearly colliding with a book cart in her haste.

On my way. Don't let them leave before I get there! And send more evidence...for research purposes.

Maria waited for more pictures to arrive as she power-walked home. Five minutes passed. Ten. Nothing.

What? No photos? she texted, slightly concerned that Emma's phone had died—or worse, that the gardeners had finished their work and departed.

Three little dots appeared, disappeared, then reappeared for an uncomfortably long time. Finally:

Yeah, that didn't go as planned.

Maria frowned. *What happened?*

The reply took another minute to arrive.

I may have got a bit too enthusiastic with the surveillance operation. I was leaning out my bedroom window for a better angle, and, well... I dropped my phone.

You dropped your phone?

Yes, I dropped it INTO THE GARDEN. Right between them. And Maria, it gets worse. I'd switched to video mode for the "enhanced experience." The video was STILL RUNNING when it landed. Facing upward. At my window. Where I was clearly visible.

Maria clapped a hand over her mouth, torn between horror and hysterical laughter.

They picked it up, Maria. THEY PICKED IT UP. And they SAW THEMSELVES on the screen. Then they looked up and saw ME. I ducked back so fast I think I pulled something in my neck.

How did you get your phone back? she typed.

'I sent Rosie to get it. She had to prise it out of the hands of the Greek god landscapers. It had about fifteen seconds of video evidence

of me, a woman old enough to collect a pension, filming them like I'm directing Magic Mike 3: Garden Edition.

Maria snorted so loudly that the man walking passed her flinched a little.

I'm going to have to leave the country. I can't stay here. I've never been more embarrassed in my ENTIRE LIFE. Not even when I got my skirt caught in my knickers at that charity lunch.

Did they say anything? Maria asked, shoulders shaking with silent laughter.

One of them RANG THE DOORBELL. I hid in the airing cupboard until they gave up.

Maria was laughing so hard now that tears were streaming down her face.

I'm going to have to hire new gardeners. And possibly wear a disguise whenever I go outside. Or we could move house. How do you feel about Scotland?

Maria wiped her eyes, struggling to type through her giggles.

I'll be home in ten minutes. Don't pack for Scotland yet.

Bring wine. ALL the wine. And possibly a paper bag I can wear over my head for the foreseeable future.

As she trundled toward home, Maria laughed to herself; 62 years old and they were still getting into the kind of mischief that would make their grandchildren blush.

THE GHOST OF MARRIAGE PAST

Maria walked into the house and smiled to herself as the aroma of burnt French toast entered her nostrils. Emma really needed a new hobby; this cooking lark didn't suit her at all and undercover filming was a no-go area.

She found Emma in the sitting room, hiding behind a newspaper that was held suspiciously high, covering her entire face.

"I come bearing lovely ginger ale," Maria announced, placing the bottle on the coffee table. "Thought it might help to calm your nerves a bit."

The newspaper lowered just enough to reveal Emma's eyes, which narrowed at Maria. "You find this hilarious, don't you?" she asked, voice muffled behind the financial section.

"Me? Amused by my sixty-two-year-old housemate being caught filming topless young men from her bedroom window? Whatever would give you that impression?" Maria sat down, unable to keep the grin off her face.

Emma finally lowered the newspaper with a dramatic sigh. "I've had to turn the front doorbell volume down. Every time it rings, I have heart palpitations thinking it's them returning with a cease and desist order."

Maria burst out laughing. "I didn't even know gardeners were coming today. Did you schedule them?"

"No," said Emma, accepting a generously filled glass. "No idea why they turned up. They must have been hired by the previous owners."

"Did you tell them the previous owners had left?"

"No, mate, I was on the floor, squirming with embarrassment and praying for death to save me," Emma said, taking a substantial gulp of her drink. "Besides, if they keep showing up randomly, who am I to correct this fortuitous misunderstanding?"

"You're incorrigible," Maria chuckled.

"I'm traumatised," Emma corrected. "I used to be respectable, you know. I managed hedge funds. Now I'm hiding from hedge trimmers."

"At least your phone survived the fall," Maria observed, nodding toward the device sitting on the table.

Emma groaned again. "It's tainted now. I can't even look at my camera app without blushing. And did I tell you they left a note: 'Maybe try landscape mode next time.'"

Maria doubled over, tears of laughter streaming down her face.

"It's a double entendre, Maria! They made a gardening pun about my humiliation!"

"You have to admit," Maria said, wiping her eyes, "they do have a sense of humour."

"Yes, well," Emma sniffed, though a smile was starting to crack through her mortification, "next time they come, I'm wearing sunglasses and a headscarf. And you're answering the door."

"Fair enough," Maria agreed, raising her glass in a toast. "To your brief but memorable career in wildlife photography."

"To getting old disgracefully," Emma countered, clinking her glass against Maria's.

"Where've you been, anyway? What could possibly have been more interesting than half-naked young men in the garden?"

"I was researching the house. It's fascinating, actually. Our house has quite a colourful history. It was built by a wealthy textile merchant and there was some sort of family scandal in the 1890s that led to them selling it suddenly."

"Ooh, scandal. Do tell," Emma leaned forward.

"Nothing definitive yet," Maria said carefully. "But I know there were two deaths - the young heir to the family fortune and a kitchen maid were poisoned. It sounds like forbidden love. I bet they were killed because they fell in love and there's no way the heir to a fortune could be seen marrying a kitchen maid."

Lisa and Rosie wandered into the room and Maris wanted to stop talking. She worried that Lisa would mock her, but Emma urged her to carry on.

"Well, everyone thought the two of them died from the same poisoning, but when I looked through all the diary entries and the funeral notices, it showed that they died two weeks apart. The guy – he's called James – he died from the poison at a family meal and the woman – Eliza, she killed herself later on, by poisoning herself because she couldn't bear to live without James."

"That's incredible," said Emma. "And they were both poisoned in here? In the house?"

"They were, and then Eliza killed herself in the attic."

"Oh my God – I live in the attic," said Rosie.

"Yes, but not actually in your room, apparently there's a sealed off bit where she was forced to live and then killed herself."

Rosie looked doubtful.

"Don't you remember when we moved in…we said your room didn't go all the way across – I bet that's because there's a separate sealed up room there."

"Christ. Well, we're not going to try and find it, if that's what you're thinking."

Maria was relieved that her historical interest wasn't being mocked, but she was disappointed that the others weren't interested in trying to find the sealed room. She was dying to go on an adventure to find it.

"You've got such a knack for research. You need a career that utilises your skills," said Lisa.

"Speaking of careers," Emma interjected, "I've been thinking about what you said yesterday, Maria, about wanting to do something meaningful. What about historic home restoration consulting? You could combine your organisational skills with your love of old houses."

As the conversation shifted to potential career paths for Maria, Lisa felt another wave of fatigue wash over her. She fought to keep her expression neutral so as not to let her friends see how quickly her energy was fading.

A loud bang on the door interrupted their chat.

"I'll get it!" Emma called out, grateful for any excuse to abandon the lunch she'd been attempting. Breakfast had been a disaster and everyone was hungry, so she'd moved on to lunch preparation instead. She stopped chopping vegetables and headed for the door, a witty greeting ready on her lips, but the words died as she saw who was standing on the doorstep. Her expression shifted from welcoming to arctic in the space of a heartbeat.

"Well, well, well," Emma drawled, her eyes narrowing. "If it isn't Derek the Deserter. To what do we owe this dubious pleasure?" She planted herself firmly in the doorway, arms crossed, a human barricade protecting her friend.

Derek shifted his weight from one foot to the other, his expensive shoes crunching on the gravel. "I'm here to see Rosie. Is she in? Or is she out with Mike?"

Before Emma could deliver the scathing retort that hovered

on her tongue, Rosie appeared behind her, her face paling at the sight of her ex-husband.

"Derek? What are you doing here?"

Derek's eyes lit up, taking in the sight of her. "Rosie! You look... you look wonderful." His gaze lingered on her face, her hair, her hands. "I was hoping we could talk. Privately," he added, with a pointed look at Emma, who showed no signs of budging from her protective stance.

Rosie hesitated, her fingers unconsciously moving to the locket around her neck – a gift from Derek on their 20th anniversary, just months before he'd left her for Pauline.

"I... I don't think that's a good idea, Derek," Rosie began, but was interrupted by Lisa's arrival on the scene. She moved more slowly than usual, one perfectly manicured hand trailing along the wall for support.

"Darling, who's at the... oh." Lisa's voice cooled noticeably as she recognised Derek. "I see the prodigal ex has returned. How quaint! I'm going upstairs for a sleep, Rosie. If you need anything, call me."

"I will. Have a good sleep."

"I will. I need to finish reading the novel. We have book club tomorrow, remember."

"I know, I haven't finished it either. See you later."

Lisa took one last glance at Derek before walking up the stairs, taking in the man's receding hairline and expanded waistline with a mixture of satisfaction and pity.

Derek's frustration was visible in the tight set of his jaw. He didn't want to hear about book club, or Lisa having a sleep or Emma's anger with him.

"Please, Rosie. Five minutes. That's all I'm asking."

Rosie looked at her friends, seeing the concern in their eyes. She squared her shoulders and nodded. "Five minutes, Derek. In the garden." She turned to Emma. "Could you put the kettle on?"

The British euphemism for 'please prepare the ceremonial beverage of confrontation' was not lost on any of them.

As Rosie led Derek to the back garden, Emma and Maria exchanged worried glances.

"I don't like this," Emma muttered, filling the kettle with more force than necessary. "That man has some nerve, showing up here."

Maria nodded in agreement, easing herself onto a kitchen stool. "Indeed. Though I must say, he's looking rather worse for wear. Seems life with the vivacious Pauline isn't all joy and passion." She paused, a smile playing at her lips. "The years have not been kind. He's been slapped around the face by karma."

Through the kitchen window, they could see Rosie and Derek standing among the blooming flowers, their body language stiff and uncomfortable. It was Derek who spoke first, gesturing to the garden around them.

"You've done wonders with the garden," he said. "It's beautiful."

"Thank you," Rosie replied stiffly. "But I doubt you came here to discuss my horticultural skills. What do you want, Derek?"

Derek took a deep breath, his chest expanding beneath his expensive shirt. "I've made a terrible mistake, Rosie. Leaving you... it was the biggest regret of my life. I miss you. I miss us. I was hoping... well, I was hoping we could try again."

Rosie felt as if the ground had dropped out from under her feet. For so long after he'd left, she had dreamed of hearing those words, had imagined this moment with desperate longing. But now, standing here, looking at the man who had broken her heart, she felt... nothing. No, not nothing. She felt strong. The weight of her pain had transformed, like coal to diamond, into something far more valuable.

"Oh, Derek," she sighed, the sound carrying on the morning breeze. "There is no 'us' anymore. You made sure of that when you walked out on thirty years of marriage for a fling with a woman half your age."

"It wasn't just a fling!" Derek protested, colour rising in his cheeks. "I thought... I thought I was in love."

Rosie's laugh was tinged with bitterness. "And now? Now that your midlife crisis has run its course, you think you can just come back and pick up where we left off? Life doesn't work that way, Derek. I've changed. I'm not the same woman you left behind. I'm not your backup plan, your safety net, or your retirement strategy."

As if on cue, the back door opened, and Emma's voice rang out across the garden. "Tea's ready. And if Derek knows what's good for him, he'll be on his way."

Derek blanched at Emma's words, taking an involuntary step back. Behind her, Maria leaned against the doorframe, her posture relaxed but her eyes watchful. She somehow managed to look both elegant and threatening despite her evident fatigue – like a Bond villain's sophisticated yet deadly assistant.

Rosie smiled at her friends' protective fury. "You'd better go, Derek," she said softly. "Please don't come back. Whatever we had... it's in the past. I've moved on. You should too."

As Derek trudged dejectedly towards the gate, his shoulders slumped in defeat, Rosie felt a weight lift from her chest. She turned to see her friends watching, their faces a mixture of concern and pride.

As soon as Derek had left, the women gathered around Rosie in the kitchen, offering hugs, tea, and in Emma's case, promises of creative revenge.

"I know a guy who can get us twenty kilos of gelatin powder, no questions asked," she assured them with disturbing confidence. "One call, and Derek's precious Audi becomes a giant jelly mould."

"Are you alright?" Maria asked, placing a comforting hand on Rosie's arm.

"I really am," Rosie said, her smile genuine. "I feel... liberated."

As the afternoon sun streamed through the kitchen windows, the conversation turned to their own past relationships, each woman reflecting on the paths that had led them to this moment.

Emma recounted the controlling nature of her ex-husband Robert, who had criticised everything from her career choices to her fashion sense. "He once told me my outfit made me look like 'a colour-blind toddler dressed a scarecrow,'" she recalled, rolling her eyes. "And I was wearing a suit! From Marks & Spencer!"

Maria spoke softly of the pain of discovering David's affair, the betrayal that had shattered her world. "I found hotel receipts in his jacket pocket," she said, twisting her wedding ring – a habit she hadn't yet broken. "When I confronted him, he didn't even have the decency to deny it. Just said he 'needed more' than I could give him."

"What a prick," Emma muttered.

"I thought I'd never trust again," Maria admitted. "But being here, with all of you... it's helped me remember who I am beyond just being someone's wife."

As they shared stories, both painful and humourous, Rosie felt a deep sense of gratitude for these women who had become her family. They had stood by her, supported her, and now, they had helped her find the strength to truly close the chapter on her life with Derek.

The conversation eventually turned to Mike, the charming doctor Rosie had been seeing for a few months. After the whirlwind of meeting him and the excitement of their early dates, he'd disappeared completely.

"I haven't heard from him in almost two weeks," Rosie admitted, her fingers worrying the edge of her napkin. "I'm starting to think I've been ghosted."

"Nonsense," Emma declared, straightening in her chair. "A

man doesn't look at a woman the way he looked at you just to disappear. There must be an explanation."

"Like what?" Rosie asked, trying to keep the hope from her voice.

"Perhaps a medical emergency," Maria suggested practically. "Or a family crisis."

"Or he's been abducted by aliens," Emma offered.

Rosie's laughter broke the tension. "To new beginnings," she said, her voice strong and clear. "And to the family we choose for ourselves."

As the evening deepened and they prepared for bed, Rosie's phone buzzed with a text. She looked down, startled to see Mike's name on the screen.

I'm so sorry for the radio silence. My mother had a stroke. I've been in Scotland at her bedside. Can we talk tomorrow? I miss you.

Rosie's heart fluttered as she typed her reply, a small smile playing on her lips.

COCKTAILS, CONFESSIONS AND CHAOS

"Are you sure about this?" Emma whispered, glancing nervously up the narrow staircase that led to the top floor. She clutched a heavy-duty torch in one hand and her mobile in the other, both held with white-knuckled intensity.

"Of course I'm sure," Maria replied, though her voice lacked its usual conviction. "Lisa and Rosie will be at their book club for at least two hours. Plenty of time to explore."

Emma sighed, adjusting her cardigan. "We should be getting lunch ready for them when they come back."

"We can do both," Maria insisted, studying the property plans she'd photocopied at the library. "According to these, there's a separate storage area adjacent to the main attic room—Rosie's bedroom. It's accessible through a different staircase. I've been studying the house's architecture, and there are several spaces that don't match up with the exterior dimensions."

"And where exactly is this mysterious second staircase?"

Maria pointed to the small door at the end of the hallway—one they'd all assumed was a linen cupboard. "Right there. It should lead up to the space next to Rosie's room."

"You mean the door I've been shoving extra towels into since we moved in?" Emma asked sceptically, but she was already moving toward it, curiosity overcoming her reluctance.

Sure enough, behind Emma's haphazardly stacked towels was a narrow staircase, winding upward into darkness. Each wooden step creaked ominously beneath their feet as they ascended, decades of settled dust puffing up with each footfall.

"This feels like the beginning of every horror film I've ever seen," Emma muttered, playing her torch beam across the dusty steps. "Next you'll tell me there's a doll that comes alive at midnight or a painting with eyes that follow you."

"Shh!" Maria hushed her, reaching the top of the stairs. They emerged into a small, dusty space with sloped ceilings—clearly part of the attic but separate from Rosie's room. Cobwebs hung from the rafters like delicate lace, and the air smelled of old wood and forgotten things.

"Charming," Emma deadpanned, sweeping her torch around. "Just needs a bit of dusting. And possibly an exorcist."

Maria consulted the plans again. "This is fascinating. According to these old blueprints, there's another space behind that wall – probably an original storage area that got sealed off during renovations over the years."

The women picked their way carefully across the attic space, through trunks and boxes left by previous owners. At the far wall, Maria ran her hands along the rough plaster, looking for any sign of a concealed entrance.

While Emma and Maria fumbled and stumbled in the attic room next to her, Rosie lay in bed, willing her phone to ring. Nope. It was no good, a watched phone never rings. She put the phone down, picked up her book and – of course – her phone rang.

"Did you hear that?" said Maria, tapping lightly on different sections of the wall. "I'm sure I heard bells ringing. Like church bells."

"I heard something," said Emma.

"There – did you hear that? A voice. I bet that's the ghost. She knows we're coming to free her."

Rosie smiled as soon as she heard Mike's voice. The familiar tone, the reassuring words.

"I'm so sorry. I should have got in touch with you. I've been thrown for six. I came up to Scotland without my phone charger and have been running around ever since."

"Sure, I understand," said Rosie. "It's a shame you couldn't have just sent a quick text or something."

"I thought that would be rude. I thought it was better to try and talk to you."

"Oh, it's fine," said Rosie, hating the sound of herself moaning like a teenager. "Don't worry. The most important thing is – how's your mum?"

"She's feeling much stronger, but still bedbound and unable to talk properly. And her memory's gone. She's like a little girl."

"Oh, I'm so sorry. How long do you think she'll be in hospital for?"

MARIA'S FINGERS paused on a section of wall that sounded hollow when tapped. "Here. There's something different about this part." She pressed against it, and to their surprise, a small section of the wall swung inward—not a proper door, but a crude access panel.

"Well, I'll be damned," Emma whispered.

Before Maria could respond, the floorboard beneath her foot gave way with a splintering crack. She lurched forward with a startled cry, instinctively grabbing for Emma but only succeeding in pulling her friend along as she tumbled through the opening in the wall.

They fell through darkness for a heart-stopping moment before landing in an ungraceful heap of limbs and muffled curses.

BERNICE BLOOM

When they'd untangled themselves and Emma had retrieved her dropped torch, they discovered they were not in a hidden chamber, but sprawled at the foot of a familiar bed.

"Listen, I'll have to call you back later, the oddest thing's just happened," she said, ending her phone call and looking and her housemates. "What the hell??"

"Rosie!" Maria exclaimed, scrambling to her feet. "You're supposed to be at book club!"

"And you're not supposed to be falling through my wall."

"No, fair point," said Maria, brushing dust from her trousers.

Emma, still on the floor, began to laugh—a high, slightly hysterical sound. "We were exploring the attic spaces. Maria has this theory, as you know."

"So you decided to test this theory by crashing through my bedroom wall?" Rosie asked, setting her book aside and swinging her feet to the floor. She was dressed in comfortable loungewear, clearly having opted for a quiet morning at home rather than discussing the latest bestseller over tea and cake.

"We thought you were out," Maria said weakly.

"I hadn't finished the book. Neither had Lisa, so we decided not to go." She squinted at them. "Now, what's all this again, what exactly are you looking for?"

Fifteen minutes and one thorough explanation later, Rosie stood with her arms crossed, surveying the section of wall where Emma and Maria had tumbled through. The rough access panel had swung shut again, blending almost seamlessly with the rest of the wall.

"So, where do you think this magical sealed room is then?"

"I bet it's beyond where we fell through," said Maria.

"Show me where you came from," Rosie said with a resigned sigh.

The three women climbed the narrow staircase at the end of the hallway, returning to the dusty storage area. Rosie grimaced at the decades of accumulated grime.

SASSY SISTERHOOD

Maria located the access panel again, and this time all three of them carefully made their way through into a narrow crawl space between Rosie's room and what appeared to be another walled-off section.

"This is like a secret passage between the walls," Emma whispered, her torch beam cutting through the darkness. "I'm genuinely creeped out now."

"Look," Maria pointed to where the crawl space opened into a larger area in the eaves. "That must be it."

The space widened enough for them to stand, though Rosie and Emma had to hunch slightly under the sloped ceiling. At the far end was a solid-looking wall with an ornate panel set into it —clearly original to the house, unlike the crude access they'd used to enter the crawl space.

"It's a proper door," Rosie murmured, reaching out to trace the decorative carvings on the panel. "Hidden in plain sight if you were in the room it opens into, but almost impossible to find from this side." Her fingers paused on a section of carving that looked identical to every other piece, but when she pressed it, there was a faint click, and the panel swung inward a few inches.

The three women froze, staring at the narrow opening.

"Well," Emma said after a long moment, her voice unnaturally high, "that's not at all terrifying."

Maria approached the panel slowly, as if in a trance. "This is it. The sealed room. Where Eliza took her own life after learning of James's death."

Maria pushed the panel further open. The hinges groaned in protest, decades of dust and disuse making them stiff. Darkness yawned beyond, and a rush of stale, cold air washed over them —air that hadn't circulated in over a hundred years.

Emma's torch beam cut through the gloom, revealing a small, perfectly preserved Victorian sitting room. A table with two place settings. Two chairs, positioned intimately close. Two wine glasses, one empty, one still containing the dried residue of its contents. A velvet ring box, open and empty

"Oh my God," Maria breathed, all scepticism vanishing. "It's real. It's all real."

"It's a tomb," Emma whispered.

The three women stood in silence, staring into the preserved moment of heartbreak from 1892.

"Let's... let's go downstairs," Rosie finally said, her voice unsteady. "I think we all need a cup of tea. Or something stronger."

Emma nodded, already backing away from the opening. "And we should close this up. For now, at least."

"What about Lisa?" Rosie asked as she carefully pushed the panel closed, the click of the latch echoing with finality. "Should we tell her?"

Emma shook her head.

"So we just... what? Pretend we didn't find a perfectly preserved Victorian suicide scene in our attic?" asked Maria.

"We need time to process this, to figure out what it means."

As they descended the stairs, the enormity of their discovery settled over Emma like a physical weight. They had found more than just a sealed room—they had uncovered tangible evidence of Maria's story which, to be frank, she hadn't really believed. She was worried that now Maria had found the sealed room she'd be more obsessed than ever with the notion on ghosts in their house.

All three women sat quietly, lost in thought.

"We need a distraction," Emma declared suddenly. "Something normal. Something to take our minds off... whatever that was up there." She gestured vaguely toward the ceiling.

"Like what?" Rosie asked, filling the kettle with shaking hands.

"A night out," Emma suggested. "Dancing, drinks, music, people. The opposite of creepy attic spaces, murder and suicide."

"That's... actually not a bad idea," Rosie admitted. "Lisa's been talking about showing us her London club scene."

"There's no way she's well enough to go out nightclubbing."

"Who's not well enough to go nightclubbing?"

"We were just thinking about a night out," Rosie said. "How do you feel about hitting the town tonight? The four of us, dressed to kill, showing London how it's done?"

Lisa's face lit up, her fatigue momentarily forgotten. "Darlings, I thought you'd never ask! I know just the place—very exclusive, very chic. The owner owes me a favour after I ghostwrote his divorce statement. It was my finest work of fiction to date."

As Lisa launched into detailed outfit recommendations, Emma caught Maria's eye across the table and mouthed, "Not a word about upstairs."

Maria nodded slightly, her gaze drifting toward the ceiling. She was preoccupied with the house's structural mysteries, but even she recognised that tonight needed to be about fun, about living in the moment rather than dwelling on the past.

By 8PM, champagne glasses were being dusted off and spectacular outfits were being shimmied into. The Sensational Sixties Squad was preparing for their first official girls' night out since moving in together, a celebration of their new living arrangement and a much-needed break from the drama of exes, ghosts, illness and everyday life. The air practically fizzed with anticipation and Chanel.

"There's something I have to tell you all," said Rosie.

Emma and Maria glanced at one another, surely Rosie wasn't going to mention the attic room.

"I had a text from Mike last night."

"Yeaaahhhhhh..." they chorused. "At last."

"I hope he had a bloody good excuse for not contacting you," said Lisa. "He's been a bit of a dick to completely ignore you."

"His mum had a stroke," said Rosie. "She lives in Scotland and he jumped in the car and headed up there."

"Yeah, I get it, but he couldn't send you a message? It would have taken him 10 seconds to let you know and it would have stopped all your worrying."

"I know. I said that to him and he just apologised. There was some story about forgetting his phone charger."

"You've spoken to him?"

"Yes, briefly, earlier today, then I had to end the call when Emma and Maria arrived in my room."

"Oh, you must be so pleased," said Maria. "I know how much you like him."

"Yes, I am, but I take Lisa's point – it doesn't show much commitment if he couldn't spend a few seconds to send a message. I'll tread with caution from now on."

In her room, Lisa carefully applied her makeup, her hand steady as she traced the perfect line of eyeliner despite her fatigue. She studied her reflection in the mirror – still beautiful, still elegant, but there was no denying the hollowness in her cheeks, the shadows under her eyes that even the most expensive concealer couldn't quite hide.

One night, she promised her reflection. One perfect night with my friends before I tell them the truth. Before everything changes.

She selected a shimmering cocktail dress that caught the light with every movement, remembering how it had once fit her curves perfectly. Now it hung a little looser, but with strategic accessories, no one would notice. Or at least, they'd be too polite to mention it.

"Are you ready?" Rosie called from downstairs. "The taxi will be here soon."

"Coming, darling!" Lisa replied, pinning on a smile as bright and dazzling as her earrings. Tonight was about celebration, about joy, about living fully in every moment. Tomorrow would bring what it would bring.

The door creaked open, and Emma stepped out, looking decidedly uncomfortable in a dress that was clearly borrowed from Lisa's extensive wardrobe. "I feel like a drag queen," she grumbled, tugging at the hemline. "If this dress were any tighter, I'd qualify as vacuum-packed leftovers. Honestly - I feel like I'm wearing a designer sausage casing. My internal organs have filed a complaint."

Lisa clapped her hands in delight, though the gesture seemed to cost her more energy than it should have. "Oh, Emma, what nonsense. You look absolutely stunning. See what a little effort can do?"

Emma rolled her eyes, but there was a hint of a smile playing at her lips. "Yeah, yeah. Just don't expect this to become a regular thing. My sweatpants are already crying themselves to sleep in my drawer. I can hear them whispering 'traitor' from here."

As they piled into the waiting taxi, the excitement was palpable. Lisa regaled them with tales of the exclusive club they were heading to, promising VIP treatment thanks to her connections in the publishing world. "The owner owes me a favor after I ghostwrote his divorce statement. It was my finest work of fiction to date."

The club, when they arrived, was a pulsing hub of music, lights, and energy. As they stepped out of the taxi, heads turned to take in the sight of four impeccably dressed women of a certain age, exuding confidence and style.

"See?" Lisa whispered to Maria, who was looking a bit overwhelmed. "They're all looking, darling. We've still got it."

"Yeah, they're all looking because they've never seen anything like it before. Grandmas' outing."

"Not at all, follow me." Lisa's name opened doors, and soon

they found themselves ensconced in the VIP area, champagne flowing freely as they took in the scene. The velvet rope parting for them like the Red Sea.

Emma, who had been sceptical about the whole affair, found herself warming to the atmosphere. "You know," she shouted over the music, "this isn't half bad. Though I still maintain that I could have worn trousers and fitted in just as well. There was no need to dress me as Baroness Glenda Glitterbum of Esher."

Rosie laughed, feeling more carefree than she had in years. "Where's your sense of adventure, Baroness? Live a little!"

As the night wore on, each of the women found themselves embracing the spirit of the evening in their own way.

Lisa was in her element, charming everyone around her with witty anecdotes and fashion advice, though her friends noticed how she needed to sit down more frequently than usual. At one point, she even managed to convince the DJ to play some classic hits from their youth, leading to an impromptu dance party that had the younger clubgoers watching in awe.

Rosie, fuelled by champagne and the infectious energy of her friends, found herself on the dance floor more often than not. She danced with abandon; her movements suggesting that whatever she lacked in contemporary dance knowledge she more than made up for with enthusiasm and impressive flexibility that belied her age.

And Emma? Emma surprised them all. Once she got over her initial discomfort, she threw herself into the night with gusto, soon becoming the centre of attention with her tales about the gardeners and her attempts to record them secretly.

As Emma regaled her new fan club with outrageous stories, Rosie nudged Lisa, who was looking increasingly pale. "Should we be worried?" she asked, nodding towards Emma and her admirers.

Lisa grinned. "Not at all, darling. Our Emma can handle

herself. Besides, a little attention never hurt anyone. It's good for the soul... and the ego."

As the night began to wind down, the women regrouped in their VIP area, flushed with excitement and more than a little champagne. "Ladies," Lisa announced, raising her glass though her hand trembled slightly, "I think we can safely say this night has been a roaring success. We came, we saw, we conquered!"

"Here, here!" the others chorused, clinking their glasses together.

Maria, her hair slightly dishevelled but her eyes sparkling, nodded enthusiastically. "I can't remember the last time I had this much fun. Though I'm fairly certain my feet will never forgive me."

Rosie smiled warmly at her friends. "That's what the Sensational Sixties Squad is all about. Supporting each other, pushing each other out of our comfort zones, and having a bloody good time while we're at it!"

As they made their way out of the club, Emma was stopped by the group of young men she'd been entertaining all night.

"Emma, wait!" one of them called out. "Can we get your number? Maybe meet up again sometime?"

Emma turned, a mischievous grin on her face. "Sorry, boys. I'm afraid this comet only passes through once in a lifetime. Cherish the memory!"

As they tumbled out of the taxi and into their home, the first light of dawn was beginning to peek over the horizon. They were exhausted, their feet ached, and they knew they'd be feeling the effects of the champagne for days to come. Tomorrow's headaches already sending advance warning signals like distant thunder.

HANGOVERS, HEADACHES AND HAZY MEMORIES

The morning after a night of revelry always has a particular quality—a unique blend of regret, disorientation, and the firm conviction that one will never, ever touch alcohol again.

And so it was on this late morning as sun streamed through the windows, its cheerful brightness at odds with the groans emanating from various bedrooms. The women were feeling the full effects of their wild night out.

Emma shuffled into the kitchen with her eyes half-closed, her hair a chaotic nest atop her head. She made a beeline for the coffee maker, muttering under her breath about the cruelty of mornings and the evils of champagne. Her hair had achieved a sculptural quality that would have earned a place in the Tate Modern's more experimental exhibitions.

"Good morning, sunshine," Rosie's voice came from the kitchen table, where she sat nursing a cup of tea and looking remarkably put-together, all things considered.

Emma grunted in response, not trusting herself to form coherent words until she'd had her first sip of coffee. A grunt that eloquently communicated 'speak to me again before caffeine and they'll never find your body.'

Maria appeared in the doorway, wrapped in a dressing gown and looking thoughtful despite her obvious hangover. "Is Lisa up yet?" she asked, accepting a mug of tea from Rosie with a grateful nod.

"Haven't heard a peep," Rosie replied. "Best to let her sleep. She was completely exhausted by the time we got home."

Emma took a long sip of coffee, then set her mug down with purpose. "So," she said, her voice still raspy from the previous night's shouting over music, "are we going to talk about the elephant in the attic?"

"That sealed room gave me the creeps," Rosie admitted, a shiver passing through her despite the warmth of the kitchen. "All those perfectly preserved things, just waiting there for over a century."

"It's like a museum exhibit," Emma agreed, "but without the helpful placards explaining why you shouldn't touch anything."

"We need to go back up there. We need to properly document what's in the room," said Maria.

"Why?" Emma asked, arching an eyebrow. "So we can confirm your ghost theory? Maria, I love you, but after sleeping on it, I'm not convinced that James Blackwood's spirit is haunting us."

"I know how it sounds," Maria conceded, "but you saw that room. You can't deny that something tragic happened in this house."

"No one's denying the tragedy," Rosie said gently. "It's a heartbreaking story. But it doesn't mean you have to believe the ghost theories."

Emma nodded in agreement. "I'm with Rosie on this."

"OK," said Emma. "But can we just go back up there once – to make a note of everything that's there, then we'll seal it up and I won't mention it again.

Rosie sighed, reaching across the table to squeeze Maria's hand. "If it makes you feel better, we can go back up and look at the room."

"Agreed," Emma said firmly.

After a quick breakfast that none of them particularly wanted but all acknowledged was necessary to help ameliorate the effects of last night's alcohol, the three women climbed the narrow staircase to the storage area adjacent to the attic. The hidden panel was exactly as they'd left it, undisturbed in its centuries-old position.

"I should have brought sage or something," Emma muttered as Maria carefully pushed the panel open. "Isn't that what people use to cleanse haunted spaces?"

"This isn't a séance, Emma," said Rosie.

The sealed room was just as eerie in the morning light as it had been the previous day. The table with its two place settings stood as a silent testament to plans unfulfilled, dreams shattered.

Maria moved carefully into the room, drawn to a small writing desk in the corner. "Look at this," she said, picking up a leather-bound journal. "It's Eliza's diary."

The other two joined her, peering over her shoulder as she carefully turned the fragile pages. The final entry, dated March 29, 1892, was written in a shaky hand:

My dearest James, They tell me you are gone, but I cannot believe it. How can the world continue when you are no longer in it? Your father has taken everything from us—our love, our future, our child. I cannot bear this emptiness.

I have set the table as we planned, with the wine we were to share in celebration. The rings that were to bind us lie ready. I will join you soon, my love, and not even death will separate us again.

Forever yours, Eliza

"Oh, God," Rosie whispered, tears welling in her eyes. "She was pregnant. She knew exactly what she was doing."

"It's unbearably sad," Maria agreed, carefully closing the diary. "She chose to die in the same place where they had planned to celebrate their elopement."

Emma had wandered to the other side of the room, examining the contents of a small wooden box. "There are letters here," she said, holding up a bundle tied with faded ribbon. "And... oh." She paused, lifting out a small, yellowed photograph. "I think this is him."

The other two gathered around. The photograph showed a handsome young man with dark hair and serious eyes.

"James," Maria murmured, taking the photograph with careful fingers. "He looks so young."

"They were both young," Rosie said softly. "Just kids, really, with their whole lives ahead of them."

The three women stood in silence for a moment, contemplating the tragic love story that had unfolded in this very room. The air felt heavy with more than just dust—with secrets and sorrows long buried but never truly forgotten.

A sudden crash from below interrupted them, followed by a cry of pain that sent chills through all three women.

"Lisa!" Rosie gasped, already rushing toward the door.

They scrambled out of the hidden room, through the storage area, and down the stairs with panic lending speed to their movements. They found Lisa at the bottom of the main staircase, crumpled in a heap, her face contorted with pain.

"Don't move," Emma ordered, kneeling beside her. "What happened?"

"I was coming downstairs," Lisa managed through gritted teeth. "Got dizzy... missed a step."

Maria was already dialling 999, but Rosie stopped her. "Call Dr. Phillips first. If it's just a sprain, an ambulance might be overkill."

While Maria made the call, Rosie and Emma carefully helped Lisa to the sofa, propping her leg on cushions. Her ankle was already swelling, an angry red mark blooming against her skin.

"I'm sorry," Lisa said, her voice uncharacteristically small. "Where were you anyway? I called but you didn't hear me."

"We were in the attic. We found a sealed room," Rosie said. "Hidden behind a panel in the storage area next to my bedroom. It looks like it's been undisturbed for over a century."

Lisa's eyes widened with interest, momentarily distracting her from her injury. "A sealed room? Like in a mystery novel?"

"Exactly like that," Emma confirmed. "Complete with tragic backstory and spooky atmosphere."

"I'm going to be honest, I thought maybe the ghost was responsible for why you're feeling so ill. When I found out about the sealed room, I thought it I opened it up the ghost would leave and you'd get better. I know you think I'm ridiculous, but that's what I thought."

"Darling Maria," Lisa said gently, reaching for her friend's hand. "I don't think you're ridiculous, I think you're very lovely."

"I didn't know you thought the ghost had something to do with Lisa's illness."

"Yeah, I know it sounds daft, but I did, for a moment there."

When Dr. Phillips's receptionist finally answered the phone, she assured Maria that the doctor would call back within the hour. While they waited, Emma fetched ice for Lisa's ankle, and Rosie prepared tea with honey.

"Tell me more about this hidden room," Lisa prompted, clearly eager for distraction from her discomfort. "Was it terribly dramatic?"

As Maria described their discovery, she found herself viewing it differently—not as evidence of supernatural activity, but as a historical treasure, a window into the past. The tragic story of James and Eliza was no less moving without the ghostly element.

"We should document everything properly," Rosie suggested. "Perhaps even contact a historical society. That room has been preserved for over a century—it could be significant."

"Just think of the book you could write about it, Lisa," Emma added. "Once you're back on your feet, of course."

Lisa's eyes lit up at the idea. "A historical mystery set in our very own house? It's perfect! I could weave in the real history with a fictional modern-day storyline. Emma you'd have to help me with all the research."

Her enthusiasm was interrupted by the telephone. Lisa answered it, her expression growing serious as she spoke with Dr. Phillips. The others fell silent, watching her face for clues.

"Yes, I understand. Thank you, Doctor."

As she hung up, she turned to the others with a grim expression. "Dr. Phillips wants to see me immediately. He's concerned about the dizzy spells combined with the fatigue. He's going to arrange for some tests at the hospital."

Lisa's momentary good spirits faded. "I'm not sure why I have to go to a hospital, though. Surely that's an overreaction."

"It's a precaution," Rosie said firmly. "Better to be thorough."

"I'll get the car," Emma volunteered, already reaching for her keys. "Maria, can you help Lisa get ready?"

As they prepared to leave, Maria cast one last glance toward the ceiling, toward the hidden room with its century-old tragedy. Whatever was happening to Lisa, she now accepted, wasn't connected to James Blackwood's ghost. Some mysteries had supernatural explanations, but others—often the most frightening ones—were rooted in the all-too-real frailties of human existence.

"Ready to forget all that for now?" Rosie asked, breaking into Maria's thoughts.

Maria nodded, turning away from the past to focus on the present, on the friend who needed them now. "Ready."

WHEN TOMORROW BECOMES MAYBE

*L*isa sat between Maria and Rosie, holding Rosie's hand, while Emma paced restlessly. "I can't just sit there waiting for the results," she said. "I feel like I need to be doing something. If this Dr Sharma makes us wait much longer, I'm going to start a fight. That should speed things up."

Lisa managed a weak smile. "Do try to behave, darling. I'd rather not be banned from the hospital if at all possible."

"Ms Mack," called a stout nurse in an unforgiving uniform. "Please follow me."

The women stood up and walked as fast as they could to catch up with the speedy nurse. "In here," she said, showing them into a small room in which there was a bed, a couple of chairs, and a concerned-looking Dr. Sharma.

"Please take a seat. Ladies, I don't think we have enough chairs, are you OK to perch on the bed?"

His face was professionally composed, but there was a gravity to his expression that made Rosie's stomach tighten.

"We come as a package deal these days," Lisa replied with a brittle smile, settling into the chair directly across from the doctor.

Dr. Sharma nodded, his eyes kind behind wire-rimmed glasses. "I have the results of your MRI scan," he said, turning his monitor slightly so they could see the images. "I'd be lying if I said it was the news we were hoping for."

Lisa's posture stiffened, but her voice remained steady. "Just tell me, please. No sugar-coating."

"The scan shows what we call a high-grade glioma." The doctor pointed to an area on the screen. "It's a type of brain tumour that forms in the supportive tissue of the brain."

The room seemed to contract around them. Maria made a small, involuntary sound. Rosie found herself leaning forward, as if proximity might somehow make the words less devastating.

"What exactly does that mean?" Lisa asked, her voice remarkably composed. "High-grade?"

Dr. Sharma folded his hands on the desk. "High-grade means the tumour cells are dividing rapidly. These tumours tend to be more aggressive than low-grade ones."

"And glioma?" Rosie asked, needing to understand, to have something concrete to grab onto in this suddenly shifting world.

"A glioma is a tumour that starts in the glial cells—the supporting cells of the brain. They don't function like neurons but are essential for neural health and function."

Lisa took a deep breath. "How bad is it? I need to know what we're dealing with."

Dr. Sharma nodded, respecting her directness.

"High-grade gliomas are very difficult tumours to treat, both due to the problems in completely removing the tumour and their resistance to radiotherapy and chemotherapy."

"Why?" Maria asked, her voice barely a whisper.

"These tumours tend to have finger-like projections that extend into surrounding brain tissue," the doctor explained. "It makes it extremely difficult to remove all the cancerous cells without damaging critical brain structures. Occasionally, the tumour can spread to the cerebrospinal fluid and spine, though we don't see evidence of that in your case yet."

"So, what does that mean? Am I going to die?"

"There are a few additional tests we need to do and some decisions to make," said the doctor, and every woman in the room noticed that he didn't say 'no'. "We need to consider the staging—that's a measure of how far the tumour has spread beyond its original site. In your case, the tumour appears to be contained to one area, but we need to look at that more carefully."

"What now then? When do I have to come back?"

"I'm recommending immediate admission. We'll run additional tests first—a functional MRI to map brain activity around the tumour, a spectroscopy to help identify the specific tumour type, and a consultation with our neuro-oncology team."

"Admission today?" Rosie asked.

"I'm afraid so. With the symptoms Lisa is experiencing—the dizziness, fatigue, and now falls—we can't risk sending her home without proper monitoring and treatment."

"Is she going to be OK?" Rosie asked.

The doctor's hesitation was answer enough. "I don't want to get ahead of the additional tests, but I need to be honest—this type of tumour presents significant challenges. Once we have the complete picture, we'll discuss all treatment options."

"Well," Lisa said finally, her voice remarkably composed, "I suppose this explains why I've been making such a hash of the Minister's memoirs. Though frankly, a brain tumour seems a rather dramatic excuse for missing a deadline."

"Lisa," Rosie began, her voice catching.

"Don't," Lisa said firmly. "No tears, no drama."

She turned to the neurologist. "How long will I need to stay?"

"At least three days for the complete diagnostic workup. I'm starting you on dexamethasone immediately—it's a steroid that will reduce swelling around the tumour and should help with your symptoms. We'll also prescribe an anti-seizure medication as a precaution."

The next few hours passed in a blur of admissions paperwork, blood draws, and the sombre process of getting Lisa settled in. The hospital staff moved with practiced efficiency, while Lisa's three friends hovered anxiously, trying to make her as comfortable as possible.

"You three should go home," Lisa insisted once she was settled. "There's nothing to be done tonight, and you all look dreadful."

"Not a chance," Emma replied, already claiming the most comfortable-looking chair in the room. "We're staying."

By evening, they had established a rotation. Emma and Maria would head home to collect necessities for Lisa's hospital stay, while Rosie remained at her bedside, then they would swap over. The following days brought a whirlwind of tests, consultations, and increasingly technical medical discussions.

On the third day, they gathered in a conference room with Dr Sharma and two other specialists—Dr. Chen, a neuro-oncologist, and Dr. Harrison, a radiation oncologist.

"We've completed our evaluation," Dr. Harrison began, his tone gentle but direct. "The tumour is a Grade IV glioblastoma multiforme. It's the most aggressive type of brain tumour."

The room seemed to shrink around them as Dr. Chen explained the standard treatment protocol: "We recommend a three-pronged approach—surgery to remove as much of the tumour as safely possible, followed by radiation therapy and concurrent chemotherapy with temozolomide."

"Surgery?" Rosie asked. "When?"

"I've scheduled the operation for Tuesday," Dr. Sharma said. "That gives us time to optimise Lisa's condition pre-operatively and complete the necessary planning scans, Lisa will be able to go home for a week, during which time she'll have several appointments at the hospital. During this time, the steroids and anti-seizure medication will have reached therapeutic levels."

"And after surgery?" Maria asked, her notebook open, pen poised as if taking detailed notes could somehow contain the horror of the situation.

Dr. Harrison explained the six-week course of daily radiation that would follow, along with the chemotherapy regimen. The words "standard of care" and "aggressive treatment" were repeated often, but they couldn't disguise the gravity of Lisa's prognosis.

"And if we do all this—the surgery, the radiation, the chemo—what then?" Emma asked, her usual irreverence giving way to a directness that matched the doctors' own.

The three specialists exchanged glances. It was Dr. Chen who finally answered. "With the standard treatment protocol, median survival for patients with glioblastoma is approximately 14 to 16 months. However," she added quickly, seeing their expressions, "there are always outliers—patients who respond exceptionally well to treatment."

"So, a year, give or take," Lisa said calmly, while her friends struggled to maintain their composure. "And without treatment?"

"Three to four months," Dr. Sharma said quietly. "But Lisa, I strongly recommend—"

"I understand," Lisa interrupted. "And I'm not refusing treatment. I just prefer to have all the facts."

With a detailed care plan, prescriptions for steroids and anti-seizure medication, and appointments scheduled for pre-surgical assessments, the four friends left the hospital. The drive home was quiet. Lisa stared out the window, lost in thought, while Emma, uncharacteristically silent, kept glancing at her in the rearview mirror. Each woman was locked in her own thoughts, the reality of Lisa's diagnosis slowly sinking in.

Terminal. The word no one had spoken hung in the air between them.

At one point, Lisa's phone buzzed with a call from her publisher. She silenced it without looking, a small but significant gesture that wasn't lost on her friends. Lisa, who had built her career on never missing a deadline, or avoiding a difficult call, was now facing the ultimate deadline.

They settled in the kitchen, their usual gathering place. Emma busied herself making tea while Rosie hovered protectively near Lisa. Maria, who had been silent throughout the drive, finally spoke.

"How are you really feeling?" she asked quietly, her typically efficient tone softened by emotion.

Lisa met her gaze steadily. "Physically? The steroids are already helping with the headaches. Emotionally?" She shrugged slightly. "I'm still processing. It's not every day one receives an expiration date."

"You've always been lucky," Emma insisted, setting the teapot down with more force than necessary. "Remember Monte Carlo? You walked away with enough winnings to buy that ridiculous hat collection. You'll be lucky again. I just know you will."

Lisa smiled faintly at the memory. "True. But I don't think the casino gods have much influence over cellular biology."

"You're too beautiful to be ill," said Maria. "Sorry – I know that sounds daft, but you are. You're too bright and shiny, and – well – beautiful."

"Thank you," Lisa said with a smile. "You do cheer me up, you lunatic…if you're not looking for ghosts or researching haunted houses, you're saying the most gorgeous, heart-warming things. You're one of a king Maria Brydon."

"I forgot your surname was Brydon," said Rosie. "I've just realised we've all got the same names as comedians. Lisa Mack, after Lee Mack, Emma Davies after Greg Davies, Maria Brydon after Rob Brydon. How weird is that?"

"But you're Rosie Brown. You're letting us down," said Lisa.

"My maiden name is Mitchell. Like David Mitchell."

"Good God, that's so odd," said Emma. "We should call a newspaper and tell them. There can't be many houses full of 60-somethings who all have the names of comedians."

"There probably aren't many households with just 60-somethings in, to be honest," said Lisa.

"It has to be a lucky sign," said Maria, casually wiping an imaginary speck of dust off the dustless table. "It has to be a sign that Lisa will get better."

"I hope so," said Lisa. "I do need to do some practical things though, just in case it turns out not to be down to luck. First, I need to contact my publisher, and someone needs to tell that dreadful Minister he'll have to find another ghost writer to mythologise his mediocre career. Then we'll need to sort out the pre-surgical appointments. I can'\t expect you all to take me every time. I can get cabs. I'll just book it all in advance so I don't forget. My mind's gone to pieces."

"I'll handle the Minister," Emma volunteered. "I've always wanted to tell a politician exactly what I think of him. And you can forget about cabs, you daft mare. We'll be taking you to every appointment, staying with you and bringing you back. We come as a team. Did we not mention that. You've got three friends here who are with you through thick and thin, whatever happens. Got that?"

Lisa nodded. She was scared to speak incase you cried. She'd never known such friendship, love and loyalty before. It made her want to live more than anything else."

"Mike," Rosie said suddenly.

"Where?"

"No – I was just thinking – he's a doctor. He might be able to help. He'll know specialists, treatments, options. Would you mind if talked about it to Mike? He has loads of friends who are surgeons. You never know...one of them might be a brain surgeon?"

Lisa's expression softened. "Of course I don't mind, darling. Worth trying every avenue, and if reconnecting with your handsome doctor is a side effect of my brain tumour, at least something good might come of this mess."

The days leading up to the surgery fell into a new rhythm. Pre-operative assessments, medication schedules, good days and bad. They took turns accompanying Lisa to her appointments, each developing their own way of helping her through the process.

Rosie became the practical one, keeping track of medications and creating a system to monitor Lisa's symptoms as instructed by the neurosurgical team. Emma appointed herself chief entertainment officer, her outrageous stories managing to draw reluctant laughs even on the worst days. Maria organised everything else, channelling her research skills into learning everything she could about glioblastoma treatment options and support services.

One afternoon, as Lisa rested in her room following a particularly exhausting pre-surgical consultation, Rosie found herself alone in the kitchen when the doorbell rang. She wasn't expecting anyone, and for a brief moment considered ignoring it—they'd had enough well-meaning friends dropping by with casseroles and awkward sympathy. But something compelled her to answer.

She opened it to find Mike standing on the doorstep, looking both professional and uncomfortable, a thick folder tucked under his arm. He wore casual clothes rather than his usual GP clinic attire, but his expression carried that same calm competence that had first drawn her to him.

"Rosie," he said, his voice softer than she remembered.

"Mike." She gripped the door frame, steadying herself.

"I came as soon as I could get away from the surgery," he said, his eyes meeting hers with an intensity that made her breath catch. "I've been talking to James—my friend from medical school who's a neurosurgeon at Royal Free. I showed him Lisa's scans. He's been incredibly helpful."

His hands tightened on the folder he was carrying. "There's a clinical trial at UCLH that might be suitable for Lisa, depending on the molecular profile of her tumour. They'll be able to test for that after the surgery. James knows the lead researcher personally."

"You came," Rosie said, unable to keep the surprise from her voice. After weeks without seeing him, his sudden appearance seemed almost surreal. "I thought... after your text, and after our call...I wasn't sure if..."

Mike shifted his weight, clearly uncomfortable. "May I come in? I've brought some information that might help Lisa."

Rosie hesitated only a moment before stepping aside. He passed close enough that she caught the familiar scent of his aftershave, bringing with it a rush of memories she'd been trying to suppress.

She led him to the kitchen, where a half-finished cup of tea sat next to her notebook filled with Lisa's medication schedule and symptom tracking.

"How is she today?" Mike asked, placing the folder on the table.

"Tired. The steroids are helping with the headaches, but they keep her awake at night. The doctors say that's normal." Rosie busied herself with the kettle, needing something to do with her hands. "Tea?"

"Please." Mike sat down at the table, opening the folder. "James reviewed her case yesterday. He says her neurosurgeon has a good reputation. The surgical approach they're planning is appropriate, but there are some additional options for after surgery that might not have been discussed yet."

Rosie set a mug in front of him and sat down across the table. "Like what?"

"There's a new immunotherapy trial that's showing promising results for glioblastoma. And some centres in the US are using tumour-treating fields—a device that creates electric fields to disrupt cancer cell division." He spread out several papers with highlighted sections. "As a GP, I don't normally deal with cases this specialised, but I've been reading everything I can find."

His dedication to helping Lisa caught Rosie off guard. "I can't believe you did all this for Lisa."

Mike looked up, his expression earnest. "It's not just for Lisa, but for you. For..." he hesitated, "for us."

The word hung between them, charged with unspoken questions.

"I understand if you're angry with me," he continued when she didn't respond. "I should have called. Texted. Something more than just disappearing."

Rosie wrapped her hands around her mug, feeling the warmth seep into her fingers. "Is your mum OK?"

Mike's shoulders sagged slightly. "She's stable now. The hospital there was understaffed, and as the only doctor in the family..." He ran a hand through his hair. "I spent every waking hour coordinating her care, arguing with consultants, arranging rehabilitation. I barely slept."

"You could have told me," Rosie said quietly. "I would have understood."

"I know that now," he admitted. "At the time, I couldn't think beyond the next hour, the next crisis. By the time things stabilised enough for me to catch my breath, weeks had passed. I felt... ashamed. I thought you'd have moved on."

Rosie was about to respond when a realisation struck her. "I haven't called Mary in days," she murmured, almost to herself.

"Mary?"

"My daughter." Rosie stared into her tea. "Since Lisa's diagnosis, I've been so focused on her care that I've barely spoken to my own daughter. Just quick texts to say I'm busy, that I'll call properly 'soon.'" She looked up at Mike, understanding dawning. "I've been doing exactly what you did."

"Crisis narrows your vision," Mike said gently. "Makes the world shrink to just what's directly in front of you."

Rosie nodded, feeling a knot of resentment begin to loosen in her chest. "Who's looking after your mum now?"

"My sister's moved in temporarily to help. That's why I could finally come back." He hesitated. "I missed you, Rosie. More than I expected to."

The simple honesty in his voice cut through her defences. "I missed you too," she admitted. "And... I could use your help with Lisa. We all could."

Mike reached across the table, his hand stopping just short of hers—offering but not presuming. "I'm here now. Whatever you need."

Rosie looked at his hand, then slowly placed hers on top of it. "Tell me more about this clinical trial."

"It's a combination therapy approach," Mike said, visibly relieved to be on safer ground. "Standard treatment for glioblastoma hasn't changed much in decades—surgery, radiation, temozolomide. This trial adds a targeted immunotherapy component. James says the preliminary results are encouraging."

"Would she qualify?"

"That depends on several factors they'll determine after surgery—tumour markers, specific genetic mutations." Mike turned a page in his folder. "I've made notes about questions you should ask her oncologist. And James has offered to consult informally if her doctors are willing."

Rosie felt the first genuine hope she'd experienced since Lisa's diagnosis. "This means a lot, Mike. That you'd do all this."

"I care about you, Rosie. And that means I care about the

people important to you." His expression became more serious. "I need you to understand something about glioblastoma, though. It's... challenging. Even with the best treatment."

"I know the statistics," Rosie said quietly. "Fifteen months, give or take."

Mike squeezed her hand. "Statistics are just numbers. They don't account for the individual. Lisa is otherwise healthy, she's getting treatment at a top centre, and she has an amazing support system. Those factors matter."

"And this clinical trial could help?"

"It could. There are no guarantees, but it offers something beyond the standard approach." He paused. "The most important thing right now is getting through the surgery successfully. One step at a time."

Rosie nodded, feeling tears threatening. For days, she'd been holding herself together, being strong for Lisa, for Emma and Maria. Having someone to share the burden with, even briefly, made her defences start to crumble.

"I don't know if I can do this," she whispered. "Watch her go through this. She's so vibrant, so full of life, and now..."

"You can," Mike said firmly. "You are. And you're not alone."

A noise from the hallway made them both look up. Lisa stood in the doorway, wrapped in her silk robe, her face pale but her eyes alert.

"I thought I heard voices," she said, her gaze moving between them. "Doctor Mike, I presume?"

Mike stood immediately. "Lisa. I'm sorry if we disturbed you."

Lisa waved a dismissive hand. "Darling, when you have brain cancer, everyone tiptoes around you, it's quite annoying." She moved to the table with the careful deliberation of someone managing fatigue. "Is that tea? And what's all this?" She gestured to the papers spread across the table.

"Mike's been consulting with a neurosurgeon friend about

your case," Rosie explained, quickly wiping away the moisture from her eyes. "He's found a clinical trial that might be suitable after your surgery."

Lisa raised an eyebrow, looking at Mike with fresh interest. "Have you indeed? Well then, Doctor, pull up a chair and tell me all about it. Spare no details—I've become quite the medical enthusiast lately."

As Mike began explaining the treatment options, Rosie watched them both—Lisa's sharp questions revealing her determination to fight, Mike's patient, thorough answers showing his genuine desire to help. Something settled in her chest, a feeling of pieces slowly coming back together.

Later, after Lisa had returned to rest and they'd made plans for Mike to speak with the entire household that evening, Rosie walked him to the door.

"Thank you," she said simply.

"I'll be back tonight with more information," he promised. "And Rosie?" He paused, his hand on the doorframe. "Call your daughter. Trust me, she'll understand."

Rosie nodded, suddenly certain that she would. "And your mother... I'd like to hear more about her, when you have time."

"I'd like that too." His smile held promise—of conversations to come, of reconnection, of moving forward together despite the uncertainty surrounding them.

As she watched him walk to his car, Rosie felt the weight on her shoulders shift slightly. Not lighter, precisely, but more evenly distributed. She closed the door and reached for her phone, scrolling to Mary's number. Crisis might narrow your vision, but it also clarified what truly mattered—and who.

LATER THAT EVENING Mike came back and chatted to all four of the women about Lisa's illness, reassuring them without giving them false hope. "She's got the best doctors, and the best chance," he said.

Lisa spoke next...suddenly bristling with intensity. "I need you to promise me something," she said. "When the time comes... no prolonged sadness, no moping about. I want you to celebrate. Open that ridiculously expensive champagne I've been saving, wear something fabulous, and tell embarrassing stories about me."

"Lisa," Rosie protested.

"Promise me," Lisa insisted. "After all, darlings, I've spent far too much time making myself memorable to have you all sitting around in dreary black looking miserable."

"And another thing," Lisa continued, sitting up straighter, a determined gleam in her eye. "I refuse to spend whatever time I have left just waiting around for treatment and test results. I have things to do, experiences to have."

"Like what?" Emma asked, leaning forward.

Lisa smiled, the same smile that had always preceded her most outrageous suggestions. "I think it's time we made a list, don't you? A proper bucket list. Because if anyone needs a bucket list, it's the woman with a terminal diagnosis."

Despite the gravity of the situation, Emma laughed. "Trust you to make even brain surgery sound adventurous."

"Oh, darling," Lisa replied, "if I'm going out, you can be damn sure I'm going out in style."

DREAMS BEFORE DEADLINE

Five days after Lisa's surgery, the neurosurgical ward at the hospital had grown accustomed to the steady presence of the three women who arrived promptly at visiting hours and departed only when firmly instructed to do so. The nurses had taken to calling them "Lisa's Army," and even the most stern-faced ward sister found herself warming to their unwavering loyalty and occasional rule-bending.

Today, they'd arrived armed with contraband pastries, fresh flowers for the windowsill, and—at Emma's insistence—a bottle of expensive cream because "hospital air is an absolute menace to one's skin."

Lisa was propped up in bed, her head wrapped in bandages, but her eyes brightened considerably when her friends entered the room. The surgery had gone as well as could be expected—they had managed to remove approximately 90% of the tumour, a result he'd described as "better than we'd hoped for." Still, the procedure had taken its toll. Lisa's usual vibrancy was muted, and she tired easily.

"Well, don't just hover in the doorway like awkward party guests," Lisa said, her voice weaker than usual but still carrying that familiar imperious tone. "Come in properly and tell me what's happening in the real world. I'm desperate for news that isn't about my blood pressure or bowel movements."

Emma snorted as she arranged the flowers. "Trust me, your current world is far more interesting. We've spent the morning arguing about whether Rosie's new cardigan makes her look like a kindly librarian or a strict headmistress."

"The correct answer is neither," Rosie said, setting down her tote bag and leaning in to kiss Lisa's cheek. "I look like Kate Moss. Now, how are you feeling today, darling?"

"Like I've had my skull cracked open and my brain rummaged through," Lisa replied dryly. "But they tell me that's entirely normal."

"Your colour is better," Maria observed, already unpacking the pastries and arranging them on the small rolling table.

"And your sarcasm is definitely returning to pre-surgery levels, which I'm taking as a good sign," added Emma.

Lisa managed a small smile. "The headaches are slightly less apocalyptic, which is something. And I managed to walk to the bathroom unassisted this morning. The nurses seemed absurdly pleased with this achievement, as if I'd completed a marathon."

"It's progress," Rosie said firmly. "And progress is what matters. Any way - you're the tough one amongst us - the high achieving, nothing fazes you, go get 'em one."

"Yeah. I wish that were true. I'm not very tough deep down. One day I'll tell you about all the things that have happened to me to make me so tough on the outside."

"Oooo..yes - do. I want to know everything. You never talk about your past."

"I promise I'll tell you everythign one day."

There was a brief, comfortable silence as they arranged themselves around Lisa's bed—Emma claiming the only proper chair, Maria perching on the windowsill, and Rosie standing like a sentinel at the foot of the bed. It had become their usual formation over the past few days.

"So," Lisa said finally, "when do I get to go home? I'm starting to develop an allergic reaction to hospital décor. Whoever decided beige and mint green were soothing colours clearly never had to stare at them for days on end."

"Dr. Sharma mentioned possibly the end of the week," Rosie replied, ever the keeper of medical information. "Depends on how your final tests come back."

"But you'll need someone with you at all times for the first couple of weeks," Maria added quickly. "We've worked out a schedule. I've typed it up, colour-coded by person and responsibility."

Lisa raised an eyebrow, wincing slightly at the movement. "Of course you have."

"We've got it covered," Emma assured her. "Between the three of us, you'll never be alone, but we promise to give you enough space that you won't be tempted to murder us in our sleep."

"I make no such promises," Lisa muttered, but her eyes were warm with gratitude.

Rosie pulled a notebook and pen from her tote bag. "Now then, we've all been talking, and we thought we'd better get cracking on this bucket list, so we have lots of fun things planned for when you get out."

Lisa's eyes brightened noticeably. "Now that is the best idea I've heard since this whole brain tumour business began. Far better than the nurse who suggested I take up meditation to 'align my healing energies.'"

"You'd be terrible at meditation," Rosie agreed with a laugh. "You can't sit still for thirty seconds without critiquing something."

"I thought we could each contribute a few ideas—things that

are manageable during your recovery and treatment," said Maria.

"Manageable doesn't have to mean boring," Emma interjected quickly.

"Yes, let's not make this a sad, gentle farewell tour. I want adventures, just ones that won't burst my stitches."

For the next hour, the hospital room buzzed with energy as they brainstormed bucket list ideas. The limitations of Lisa's condition actually sparked their creativity, forcing them to think beyond conventional adventure activities.

"I've always wanted to sleep under the stars," Lisa admitted, surprising them all. "Proper stargazing, somewhere far from city lights."

"That's doable," Maria said, making notes. "We could rent a cottage in the countryside once you're stronger. Maybe the Lake District or the Cotswolds."

"I'd like to learn to paint," Rosie contributed. "Not just paint-by-numbers, but proper landscapes and portraits."

"Ooh, we could hire an instructor to come to the house," Emma suggested. "Have our own private art class. I could finally fulfil my lifelong ambition to paint nude models." She waggled her eyebrows suggestively.

"Your ambition or the model's nightmare?" Maria quipped, but she added it to the list.

"I'd like to trace my birth parents," Lisa said quietly, smoothing the hospital blanket with her hand. "I've always wondered, but there never seemed to be a right time. Now time is the one thing I'm short of." The words hung in the air, stark but without self-pity.

Maria reached for Lisa's hand. "I'll help. Between my organisational skills and Emma's complete disregard for privacy boundaries, we'll find them."

"Hey!" Emma protested, then shrugged. "Actually, that's fair."

"What about you, Emma?" Rosie asked. "What's on your bucket list?"

Emma's eyes gleamed. "I want to go skinny dipping, I want to learn everything there is to know about cheese and – yeah – I'd like to do art again."

"I love it," said Lisa. "Add it to the list, Maria."

As Maria reluctantly added "skinny dipping" to her neat list, Rosie looked thoughtfully at Lisa. "You mentioned once that you've always wanted to see the Northern Lights. That might be difficult with your treatment schedule, but what about a planetarium? They can project the aurora, and it would be warm and comfortable."

Lisa's eyes lit up. "That's brilliant, Rosie. All the beauty without the frostbite."

"I've always wanted to learn a new language," Maria admitted. "Something exotic."

"Like what? Klingon?" Emma teased.

"I was thinking more along the lines of Italian," Maria replied with dignity. "The language of art and opera and incredible food."

"Speaking of food," Lisa said, pushing away the untouched hospital lunch tray, "I want a proper food tour. Not necessarily travelling—I know that might be difficult—but experiencing cuisines I've never tried before."

"We could do a world food tour right in London," Rosie enthused. "One country each week—the restaurants, the cooking techniques, maybe even lessons from chefs."

The ideas continued to flow—some practical, some outrageous, all infused with a sense of urgency and purpose that transformed the sterile hospital room into a space of possibility and hope.

"Wine tasting!" Emma declared.

"A weekend at a luxury spa," from Rosie.

"Seeing all of Shakespeare's plays," was Maria's contribution.

"Publishing some fiction under my own name," Lisa said softly. "Even just a small poem or short story. Something that's truly mine. I love the grittiness of non-fiction, but how glorious it would be to write fiction."

Eventually, a nurse appeared to check Lisa's vitals, eyeing the half-eaten contraband pastries with amused disapproval and taking in the flowers that were banned in patients' rooms because of bacteria in the water.

"I see the party committee has arrived," she commented as she recorded Lisa's blood pressure.

"More of a dream committee today," Lisa replied with a smile.

When the nurse left, Lisa regarded her friends with a more serious expression. "There's one more thing I'd like to add to the list, but it's a bit macabre."

The others exchanged concerned glances.

"I'd like to plan my own funeral," Lisa continued. "Not in a morbid way, but... I want it to be a celebration, not a dreary affair. And I'd like the three of you to help me plan it."

A heavy silence fell over the room.

"Oh, don't look so horrified," Lisa chided. "People plan weddings all the time—why not plan the other big ceremony of one's life? Besides, it'll be fantastic. I'm thinking champagne, inappropriate anecdotes, and absolutely no black clothing allowed."

Emma was the first to recover. "I call dibs on the inappropriate anecdotes. I've got enough material to scandalise even the most liberal vicar."

"Of course you do," Maria murmured, but she was smiling despite herself.

"And I want you all to promise me something," Lisa continued, her expression growing serious. "After I'm gone—don't stop the bucket list. Keep adding to it. Keep living adventures for both yourselves and a little bit for me too."

Rosie's eyes filled with tears, but she nodded firmly. "We promise."

"Enough of this sentimental talk," Emma declared, wiping suspiciously at her own eyes. "Let's get back to planning the scandalous parts of this bucket list. I was thinking we could all get tattoos!"

"Emma!" Maria gasped. "Lisa can't get a tattoo during cancer treatment!"

"Actually," Lisa mused, "a small one might be possible during the break between surgery recovery and radiation. I've always fancied a discreet butterfly somewhere interesting."

"See?" Emma said triumphantly. "This is why Lisa's my favourite."

The planning continued until Lisa began to tire, her responses becoming slower, her eyelids drooping despite her obvious enjoyment of the conversation.

"We should let you rest," Rosie said, noticing the signs of fatigue. "We'll bring the list tomorrow, all typed up and organised."

"And with all my inappropriate suggestions included, no matter how much Maria tries to edit them out," Emma insisted.

Lisa smiled sleepily. "I love you all, you know. Even when you're being ridiculous. Especially when you're being ridiculous. Oh, and add Paris to the list – put that at the top, next to the nude models."

The three friends took one last look at their sleeping fourth member before quietly leaving the room. In the corridor, they huddled together, the reality of Lisa's condition hitting them anew now that they were away from her brave face.

"We're really going to do this, aren't we?" Emma said. "Turn even this into an adventure."

"That's our Lisa," Rosie replied, her voice thick with emotion. "Always finding the excitement, even in the grimmest situations."

"She might live for years though, mightn't she? I know she's talking about organising her own funeral, but if the chemo and radiation are successful, she might have years and years," said Maria.

"Yes, and then we'll keep doing the bucket list for years."

"She could get better. She could out-live all of us."

"Yes, she could," said Rosie, gently.

As they left the hospital and stepped into the bright afternoon sunlight, there was a new sense of purpose among them. The bucket list wasn't just a series of activities—it was a promise to Lisa and to each other that whatever time remained would be filled with joy, adventure, and the kind of memories that outlast even the most determined mortality.

On the way home, Mike called Rosie's mobile. Despite the circumstances, her heart skipped a beat when she saw his name on the screen.

"I've been consulting with some colleagues at the Royal Marsden," he said after asking about Lisa. "They're running a specialised treatment approach for cases like Lisa's. I can set up an introduction if you'd like."

"That would be wonderful," Rosie replied, gripping the phone tightly. "Mike, I... thank you. For being here. For helping."

There was a pause before he answered. "I'm not going anywhere, Rosie." The warmth in his voice wrapped around her like a promise. "I know I didn't handle things too well. But if there's one thing these past weeks have taught me, it's that life's too short to waste."

As Rosie hung up, she caught Emma watching her in the rearview mirror, one eyebrow raised in a knowing look.

"Not a word," Rosie warned, though she couldn't keep the smile from her face.

"Wouldn't dream of it," Emma replied, her eyes twinkling. "Though I might just add 'Rekindling romance with handsome doctor' to our collective bucket list."

"And I might add 'learn how to be a complete pervert and video handsome young men without throwing the recording device at them." And for the first time since Lisa's diagnosis, they all laughed together—not the strained, polite laughs of people trying to be brave, but genuine laughter that bubbled up from somewhere deep and true. It was a small moment of normal in the midst of their new reality, a reminder that joy could still be found even in the darkest times.

That evening, they sat around the kitchen table, surrounded by coloured pens, paper and the notes they'd made in hospital about the bucket list.

"Art class with nude model," Emma read aloud, grinning. "I still think we should go for the full monty. Nothing says 'seize the day' like a completely naked stranger in your living room."

"I'm not sure what the neighbours would say," Maria mused, though there was a gleam in her eye that suggested she wasn't entirely opposed to the idea.

" Gerald and Barbara Fitch from across the street would have a conniption," Rosie laughed. "Which, frankly, might be worth it just for the entertainment value."

"Well," Emma said, raising her glass of wine, "here's to the beginning of the bucket list summer. May it be filled with inappropriate nude models, smelly cheeses, Paris trips and other weird things."

"To Lisa," Rosie added softly.

"To us," Maria finished.

THE NAKED TRUTH

The morning light streamed through the bay windows lighting the impromptu art studio that had been created in the sitting room. Drop cloths covered their lovely Persian rug, easels stood in line as if awaiting orders, and the scent of oil paints and turpentine permeated the air.

"I'm looking forward to this," said Emma. "I haven't touched a paintbrush in years I'm really excited."

"You're a super brilliant artist. I can't wait to see your painting, unfortunately, the last time I did anything artistic was when I was at school and it was mainly to flick paint at Frankie Gower," said Maria.

Rosie smiled, arranging the last of the art supplies on a side table. "I'm so please we're doing this. The first item on the bucket list, and it involves us leering at a naked man."

"Old Gerald across the street might have a coronary if he glances through our windows today. He seemed excited enough when he saw me in the library, I don't know how he'll cope with nudity in the morning."

As if on cue, the doorbell rang. Maria nearly dropped the jar she was holding. "That'll be the instructor. And the... model."

Emma rubbed her hands together with glee. "Well, let's not keep the gentleman waiting. I'll get the door."

When she returned moments later, she was accompanied by a slender woman with a messy bun and paint-splattered overalls, and an attractive man who looked vaguely familiar. He had the confident air of someone comfortable in his own skin— which was fortunate, given that he would soon be displaying rather a lot of it.

"Ladies, this is Simone, our instructor, and Alejandro, our model," Emma announced, looking decidedly pleased with herself. The guy was very familiar. She wondered whether he was famous, or something. An out of work actor?

Lisa sat up on the sofa where she'd been resting, her eyes sparkling with more energy than they'd seen in weeks. "Well, well," she murmured, suddenly looking far more interested in art than she had been moments before. "I think I'm going to enjoy this class immensely. Hey – don't we know you?"

"I don't think so," said Alejandro with a deep, sexy Italian accent.

Simone clapped her hands together. "Right then! Let's get started. Alejandro will pose for fifteen minutes at a time, with five-minute breaks between. We'll begin with some quick gesture drawings to warm up, are we all here?"

"We're just waiting for Rosie. Ah, here she comes now…"

As Alejandro disappeared behind a makeshift screen in the corner to prepare, the women took their places at the easels. Rosie fussed with her smock, Maria tested different pencils with scientific precision, and Emma slouched on her stool, looking both sceptical and amused. Lisa, still too weak for prolonged standing, had been set up with a special table arrangement near the sofa.

When Alejandro emerged, wearing nothing but a strategically placed cloth, there was a collective intake of breath.

"Sweet mother of mercy," Emma muttered under her breath. "I should have paid more attention in art class."

"Less talking, more drawing," Simone instructed, moving around to adjust their postures and guide their hands. "Observe the lines of the body, the interplay of light and shadow. Don't get caught up in details yet—feel the movement, the energy."

They worked in silence for a while, each woman absorbed in the challenging task of translating the human form onto paper. The only sounds were the scratching of pencils, the occasional instruction from Simone, and Emma's barely suppressed giggles whenever the instructor used phrases like "notice the firm curve" or "pay attention to the strong line of the buttocks."

About twenty minutes into the class, Maria glanced up from her meticulous rendering and noticed movement at the window. "Um, I think we have an audience," she said quietly.

The others looked up to see Barbara Fitch from across the street, gardening shears in hand, staring open-mouthed through the window. She wasn't alone. Gerald was hovering nearby and the postman had also stopped in his tracks, drawn by the unusual sight.

"I'll shut the blinds," Emma said.

"Oh, let them look," Lisa declared, waving her paintbrush airily. "Maybe they'll learn something about art appreciation."

Simone, unperturbed by the growing audience, continued with her instruction. "Now, let's move on to shading. Notice how the light caresses the muscles here," she demonstrated on her own paper, "creating this lovely shadow beneath the testicles."

Emma glanced at Maria and they both tried not to laugh like children in a school assembly. Despite the distractions—both internal and external—they gradually became absorbed in their work. Emma, in particular, found herself lost in the challenge of capturing Alejandro's form. The minutes stretched into hours, punctuated by Alejandro's breaks, during which he donned a robe and strolled around to view their progress.

"You have a good eye," he told Emma, peering at her accomplished rendering. "You've captured the tension in the pose. You are artist, no?"

"Yes, I used to be," said Emma.

"Bellissimo."

"And you?" he said, stopping behind Rosie's easel. She looked up at him.

"Hang on, isn't your name John Collins? Didn't we meet you in the pub?"

"No, I am Alejandro and I come from Italy," he said, the accent suddenly thickening to almost comical proportions.

Emma narrowed her eyes, pencil suspended mid-air. "Yes we did. Oh my God – that's where we know you from."

"No, I from Milano," he replied.

Rosie set down her charcoal, squinting at their model. "No, I'm positive. You're that bloke from the pub. John Collins.

"I... that is..." Alejandro/John's accent began to slip noticeably.

Maria snorted. "Come on, John. You're about as Italian as fish and chips."

"Mamma mia," Emma deadpanned.

John's shoulders slumped in defeat, his accent vanishing entirely. "Alright, fine. Yes, I'm John Collins from the pub. The Italian bit just... well, it pays better, doesn't it? Women expect exotic models, not blokes named John who are recently retired. Just – please – don't tell any of the guys in the darts league at the pub – I'll never hear the end of it."

The women all laughed. "Of course we won't," they said.

"Thanks. The Italian persona was Simone's idea, actually."

All eyes turned to Simone, who gave a sheepish shrug. "It's true. My clients expect a certain... ambiance. And John Collins doesn't exactly scream 'Renaissance masterpiece.'"

"So all those Italian phrases you've been throwing around," Emma said, turning back to John. "What were those, exactly?"

"Mostly pasta names," John admitted. "And football players."

"I thought 'Penne Rigatoni del Baggio' sounded a bit suspect,'" Maria said.

Lisa was now laughing so hard she had to lie back on her chaise. "So we've spent the last two hours drawing a guy from the pub who's been pretending to be a sultry Italian named after the Spanish version of Alexander?"

"Well, I don't know about everyone else," Rosie said, trying and failing to keep a straight face, "but I think it adds an interesting dimension to the art. Drawing someone you might see playing darts on Monday while pretending he's Michelangelo's David."

"Darling, this is the most entertainment I've had since my diagnosis," Lisa declared. "Besides, you have a surprisingly good form for someone who spends their days hunched over a desk and their evenings hunched over a bar."

"Yoga," John said with a hint of pride. "Twice a week."

"Well, then," Simone clapped her hands, trying to regain control of her class. "Shall we continue? Perhaps with a new pose, Alej— er, John?"

"Actually," Emma said thoughtfully, "I think it might be good to finish things there, we've had a great time."

As the women laughed, and the myth of the Italian stallion was destroyed, Simone announced the end of the class. Alejandro disappeared to dress, and the women surveyed their work with varying degrees of satisfaction.

"Well, that was enlightening," Rosie declared, stepping back to view her artistic creation with a critical eye. "I've confirmed that Picasso I am not."

"I think we all learned something," Maria agreed, carefully cleaning her brushes. "Though I'm not sure it was entirely about art."

They gathered in the garden later that day, their paintings propped against chairs for a makeshift exhibition. The light was fading, but the warmth of the day—the laughter, the learning, the shared experience—lingered.

"To art," Emma proposed, raising her glass. "And to magnificent male specimens who inspire it."

"To art," the others echoed, clinking glasses.

"Next on the list," Lisa announced, "is the cheese tasting. I hope your palates are as adventurous as your artistic sensibilities."

Emma groaned theatrically. "If it's anything like today, the neighbours will need smelling salts."

Lisa's laugh, bright and genuine, floated up into the darkening sky. "One can only hope, darling. One can only hope."

CHEESY MOMENTS

"*R*oquefort is not meant to be that colour," Emma declared, eyeing the plate of cheeses with deep suspicion. "I'm fairly certain cheese that blue is attempting to communicate with alien life forms."

The dining room table was covered with a pristine white cloth and laden with an impressive array of cheeses—from creamy Brie to pungent Époisses, crumbly Stilton to aged Comté. Accompanying them were artisanal crackers, fresh fruits, nuts, and several bottles of wine specially selected for pairing.

"Don't be such a philistine," Lisa chided, though her eyes sparkled with amusement. "Roquefort is one of the world's great cheeses. The blue veins are Penicillium roqueforti, a specific mould that gives it that distinctive flavour."

"You're not selling it by calling it 'mould,' darling," Emma replied, gingerly placing a tiny piece on a cracker.

Maria, who had approached the cheese tasting with the same methodical precision she applied to everything, was reading all the little cards next to the cheeses. "The Camembert has notes of mushroom and grass," she murmured. "Fascinating."

Rosie, meanwhile, was in her element. Having arranged for the local cheese shop to deliver this extravaganza and teach her a little about the varieties, she was now showing off the array before them, from mildest to strongest.

"Start with a small piece of Brie," she said, exactly as the man from the cheese shop had demonstrated. "Let it come to room temperature on your tongue. Notice the texture, the initial flavour, and then how it develops."

Lisa, seated at the head of the table in what they'd all come to think of as her throne, watched her friends with undisguised affection. Though thinner than she'd been before her diagnosis, she looked almost regal tonight in a silk blouse the colour of burgundy wine, her dark hair styled in soft waves, her makeup carefully applied to bring colour to her pale cheeks.

"I had no idea you were such a cheese connoisseur, Rosie," she remarked, savouring a slice of aged Gouda. "Hidden depths, my dear."

Rosie smiled. "I admit that I've cheated – I got the cheese shop man to run through them all. But Derek and I did spend a summer in France years ago. We toured cheese-making regions, learned about affinage—the art of aging cheese. It was before the children came along."

"And before Derek became a complete two-timing plonker," Emma added, her face contorting dramatically as she braved the Roquefort. "Good lord, this tastes like someone's gym socks!"

"Actually, that's not far off," Maria observed, consulting her cheese notes. "Many blue cheeses share molecular compounds with certain foot bacteria."

"And on that appetising note," Lisa laughed, "perhaps you should move on to the wine pairings, and I'll have some of that apple juice."

The evening progressed with increasing merriment as they worked their way through the cheese board and several bottles of excellent wine. Emma, having dramatically declared the

Roquefort "an assault on humanity," discovered a surprising affinity for the creamy, ash-covered Humboldt Fog while Maria loved the goats cheese samples. Rosie glowed with the success of her carefully planned event. And Lisa, though she ate little and drank nothing, smiled throughout.

"Tell us why you wanted a cheese party on your list?" Emma asked, during a brief pause in their tasting adventure.

"It wasn't really about cheese. I wanted to experience... intensity. Of flavour, of sensation. When you're on cancer treatment, your taste buds aren't as keenly tuned. In fact, most of the time I can't taste anything. I wanted big, highly flavoured cheeses, just to taste something again."

A thoughtful silence fell over the table, broken only when the doorbell rang.

"That'll be our next surprise," Rosie said, rising to answer it.

She returned moments later, accompanied by four elegantly dressed musicians carrying instrument cases. "Ladies, meet the Halcyon String Quartet. They'll be providing the musical portion of our evening."

"You arranged a private concert?" Maria asked, impressed.

"Lisa mentioned once that she'd always wanted to hear chamber music in an intimate setting," Rosie explained. "And since we can't take her to the concert hall easily..."

"You brought the concert hall to me," Lisa finished. "Rosie Brown, you wonderful, thoughtful woman."

The musicians set up and the women arranged themselves comfortably to listen. Rosie had moved a chaise longue near the best spot for acoustics, ensuring Lisa would be comfortable. Emma sprawled in an armchair, her legs draped over one arm. Maria perched on the edge of the sofa, back straight, hands folded in her lap as if attending a formal recital. Three of them held fresh glasses of wine.

As the first notes of Mozart's String Quartet No. 19 filled the room, a hush fell over the group. The music washed over them

—sometimes playful, sometimes profound, always beautiful. In the gentle lamplight, with the lingering scents of cheese and wine, surrounded by friends, the moment achieved a certain perfection.

Lisa closed her eyes, letting the music carry her. Despite the pain that was her constant companion now, despite the knowledge of what lay ahead, this moment was a gift—one she would have treasured even without the shadow of her diagnosis. Perhaps even more because of it.

The program continued with Debussy, and concluded with a moving rendition of Schubert's "Death and the Maiden" quartet. As the final notes faded into silence, none of the women moved, each lost in her own thoughts and emotions.

Finally, Emma spoke. "Well, that was... unexpected."

"The Schubert?" Maria asked.

"No, the fact that I actually enjoyed classical music," Emma clarified. "I always thought it was just background noise for posh dinner parties."

"It's like the cheese," Rosie observed thoughtfully. "You need to give yourself time to really experience it."

After the musicians had packed up and departed, the women remained in the living room, reluctant to break the spell of the evening. The cheese board had migrated from the dining room to the coffee table, and they nibbled as they discussed the music.

"We've done the art class, now the cheese and music. What's next?" Lisa asked, her tone deliberately light. "This really is a most wonderful way to spend loads of time together.

"I believe 'Paris Evening' is next on the schedule," Maria replied. "I know that's one you were keen to do, and I don't think the hospital will let us take you to Paris."

"No, they definitely won't. Let's do Pais here then," Lisa said. "I'm glad we're doing that next. I'd like to do it on a good day, though. Maybe give me a few days to get over this. Maybe next week. On a good day."

No one wanted to acknowledge the elephant in the room—that Lisa's "good days" were becoming fewer, that the treatment was taking a harsh toll, that the prognosis remained stubbornly grim.

Lisa sat curled in the corner of the sofa, a cashmere throw pulled around her shoulders despite the warmth of the room. The soft glow of a single lamp cast long shadows across the walls, creating a pocket of intimacy in the late hour.

Emma, Rosie, and Maria had stayed up with her, their conversation meandering through memories and mundane matters, none of them quite ready to end the evening. They'd been doing this more often lately—these quiet nights together, talking about everything and nothing. Tonight, though, a different energy hummed beneath the surface of their usual banter.

"Would anyone like more tea?" Maria asked, already half-rising.

Lisa shook her head. "No, thank you. I'm fine." Her voice sounded thin, even to her own ears.

A silence fell between them, not uncomfortable but weighted with unspoken thoughts. Lisa's fingers traced the pattern on the throw, her gaze fixed on some point beyond the room.

"I had a phone appointment with Dr. Sharma today," she said finally, breaking the silence. "He's adjusted my medication again."

The others exchanged glances, knowing better than to interrupt. Lisa had been so controlled throughout her illness, recounting medical updates with the same detached precision she once used to dissect political memoirs.

"He asked me how I was coping," she continued, a slight tremor in her voice. "Mentally, I mean. I told him what I've told all of you—that I'm fine, that I'm dealing with it, that I'm not afraid."

She looked up suddenly, her eyes glistening in the low light.

"I lied," she whispered. "I've been lying to all of you. To myself."

"Lisa..." Rosie began, but Emma touched her arm gently, silencing her.

"I'm terrified," Lisa admitted, her voice breaking on the word. "Absolutely terrified. Not just of the pain or the decline—though God knows that's frightening enough—but of... ending. Of simply not being anymore."

The tears she'd been holding back for months finally spilled over, tracking silently down her cheeks. None of them had ever seen Lisa cry, not even when she'd first received her diagnosis.

"I've spent my entire life in control. Planning, organising, making things happen exactly as I wanted them to. And now there's this... this thing inside me that I can't control, can't negotiate with, can't outsmart."

Emma moved to sit beside her, taking her hand. "You don't have to be brave for us, you know."

"But I do," Lisa insisted. "Because if I'm not brave, if I let myself feel all of this..." She gestured vaguely. "I'm afraid I'll drown in it."

Maria leaned forward, her usual practicality softened by compassion. "Feeling afraid doesn't make you weak, Lisa. It makes you human."

"And you're allowed to be human with us," Rosie added quietly. "Of all people."

Lisa looked at each of them in turn, these women who had somehow become more important to her than she'd ever intended to allow. "I keep thinking about all the things I meant to do. The places I never saw, the books I never wrote." She paused, swallowing hard. "The connections I never made."

"Like what?" Emma prompted gently.

Lisa took a deep breath. "My birth mother," she said. "I always told myself I'd look for her someday. That there was plenty of time." A bitter laugh escaped her. "Turns out 'someday' has an expiration date."

"You've never mentioned wanting to find her before," Rosie said, surprised.

"I buried it, I suppose. Convinced myself it didn't matter." Lisa wiped her tears with the heel of her hand. "But now, facing the end... it feels like the most important thing I never did."

"What do you know about her?" Maria asked, and Lisa could almost see the wheels turning in her methodical mind, already planning, researching.

"Not much," Lisa admitted. "I had this whole narrative in my head growing up—that I was born in Majorca, that my mother was Spanish. It explained my Mediterranean colouring." She smiled faintly. "Turns out that was all nonsense. My adoptive parents loved Majorca, went there every year, but I was born right here in the UK."

"And your birth mother?" Emma prompted.

"Greek, apparently. That's where the Mediterranean looks come from. The adoption agency told me that much when I inquired in my thirties. But I never followed through." Lisa's fingers tightened around Emma's. "She could still be alive. Or not. I'll never know now."

"Why didn't you look for her?" Rosie asked gently.

Lisa was quiet for a moment. "Fear, mostly. Fear she wouldn't want to be found. Fear she'd be disappointed in what I'd become. Fear I'd be disappointed in her." She shook her head. "Ridiculous reasons, in retrospect."

"It's never ridiculous to be afraid," Maria said.

"But it is ridiculous to let fear stop you from the things that matter," Lisa countered. "That's what I've done. And now..." She made a helpless gesture. "Now it's too late."

The four women sat in silence, the ticking of the grandfather clock marking the passage of precious time. Outside, a light rain began to fall, tapping against the windows like gentle fingers.

"It's never too late until it's too late," Emma said suddenly, a familiar determination in her voice. "And you're still here, aren't you?"

"Emma," Rosie cautioned, her tone gentle but warning.

"No, I mean it," Emma insisted. "If finding your birth mother is what you want, Lisa, then that's what we should focus on. Not someday. Now."

"It would be like looking for a needle in a haystack," Lisa protested weakly. "I don't even know her name."

"I tracked down my ex-husband's secret offshore accounts with less information," Emma said with a wave of her hand. "And Maria can find anything with enough spreadsheets."

Despite herself, Lisa felt a flicker of something she hadn't allowed herself to feel in months: hope.

"You would do that?" she asked, her voice small.

"Of course we would," Rosie said firmly. "Whatever you need, whatever will bring you peace—that's what matters now."

"We're not giving up," Maria agreed. "Not on treatments, not on time, and certainly not on finding your mother if that's what you want."

For the first time since her diagnosis, Lisa let herself be held as she cried—really cried—the deep, body-shaking sobs of fear and grief and relief she'd been holding back for too long. Her friends surrounded her, their presence a fortress against the darkness.

Later, as the storm passed both outside and within, Lisa felt strangely lighter. The fear wasn't gone—it would never be gone—but it was shared now, divided among four hearts instead of crushing one.

"I don't know if we'll find her in time," she said softly. "But thank you. For being willing to try. For..." She gestured around the room, at the four of them together. "For all of this."

"That's what family does," Rosie said simply. "And we are your family, Lisa. By choice, which is the strongest kind."

As Lisa drifted off to sleep that night, her mind was filled not with the usual shadows of fear, but with possibilities—of connections yet to be made, of questions that might still find answers. Of precious time that, however limited, could still hold meaning and discovery.

For the first time in months, she looked toward tomorrow with something other than dread.

"Sleep well," Rosie replied, smoothing Lisa's covers with gentle hands. "Dream of cheese and Mozart."

Left alone, Lisa gazed out her window at the star-scattered sky. Whatever time she had left—weeks, months, perhaps even the year the doctors had hesitantly suggested might be possible with aggressive treatment—she would spend it like this: surrounded by beauty, by friendship, by experiences that nourished the soul.

As she drifted toward sleep, the melodies of the evening still echoing in her mind, Lisa smiled. Tomorrow would bring what it would bring—pain, perhaps, or weakness, or another round of treatments. But it would also bring friendship, and laughter, and love. And that, in the end, was what mattered most.

THE SEARCH FOR SARAH

"*She's* asleep," Rosie whispered, carefully closing Lisa's bedroom door and rejoining Emma and Maria in the garden. The three women had been taking turns sitting with Lisa since the news that things hadn't gone well with the treatment, each developing their own ways of providing comfort without smothering her with attention.

Emma pushed a mug of tea toward Rosie as she sat down. "Good. She needs the rest."

"What she needs is a miracle," Maria said quietly.

"I've been thinking," Rosie began hesitantly, stirring her tea. "Lisa mentioned something the other night that's been bothering me. About regrets."

Emma raised an eyebrow. "We all have regrets. That's what happens when you've lived as long as we have."

"Yes, but this was specific. She said her biggest regret was never finding her birth mother." Rosie looked up at the others. "What if we could give her that? Before..." She couldn't finish the sentence.

"Find her birth mother?" said Maria.

"Between the three of us, we have connections, resources, and most importantly, time on our hands," said Emma.

"Not to mention pure stubbornness," Rosie added with a small smile.

"Where would we even start?" Maria asked, but she was already flipping to a fresh page in her notebook, unable to resist a project that required organisation.

"Lisa keeps a box of documents in her closet. I've seen it when I was helping her sort through clothes for hospital stays," Rosie said. "Birth certificate, adoption papers, letters from the agency."

"Snooping through her things?" Emma asked, though her tone suggested admiration rather than censure.

"Not snooping," Rosie defended. "She showed me once, after that documentary about adopted children finding their birth parents. She said she was going to try and find hers."

"My cousin Judith works at the records office in Manchester. But..." Maria's expression grew serious. "We need to consider whether this is really what Lisa would want. Finding a birth parent can be... complicated."

"She said it was her biggest regret," Rosie repeated softly. "I think that's our answer."

The three women looked at each other, silently acknowledging the unspoken truth hanging over them: time was running out. If they were going to do this, it had to be now.

"CROSS-REFERENCE THESE DATES WITH THESE LOCATIONS," Maria instructed, passing a stack of papers to Emma. Their kitchen table had transformed into command central, covered with documents, laptop computers, and multiple notebooks filled with Maria's meticulous handwriting.

"I'm enjoying doing detective work," Emma said. She'd thrown herself into the search with surprising dedication, even calling in favours from old colleagues in the financial sector to access databases that might hold clues.

"Better than watching daytime telly," Rosie said, entering the kitchen with several heavy books from the library. "Records of regional adoption agencies, 1950-1960," she announced, setting them down. "The librarian thought I was researching a historical novel."

It had been three days since they'd begun their search. Three days of ensuring Lisa never suspected what they were doing.

"I think I might have something," Maria said suddenly, straightening up from where she'd been hunched over her laptop. "Lisa's original birth certificate listed her mother as 'Sarah J. Thompson, age 19,' but no address. I've been cross-referencing that name with women of the right age in Coventry, the area where Lisa was born."

Emma and Rosie crowded behind her, peering at the screen.

"There were fourteen Sarah Thompsons in the region at that time," Maria continued, "but only three with the middle initial J. One died in 1982, another would be too old now—she was born in 1932, not 1941 as we'd expect. But the third..."

"Sarah Jane Thompson," Rosie read over her shoulder. "Born 1941 in Birmingham. I thought Lisa was born in Coventry."

"Exactly," Maria said. "Very near."

"Does she still live there?" Emma asked, reaching for her own laptop.

"That's what I'm trying to find out," Maria replied. "According to this, she married a guy called Robert Wilson and they appear to have moved to Eastbourne. Sarah and Robert Wilson lived at 24 Seaview Road until 2010, when Robert died. After that, the trail goes cold."

"Not necessarily," Emma said, typing rapidly. "Social media, ladies. The modern detective's best friend." She turned her screen toward them. "Sarah Wilson, née Thompson, moved to a retirement community in Brighton after her husband's death.

She has a Facebook account, mostly posts about her garden and her book club."

"That could be anyone," Rosie cautioned. "How do we know it's Lisa's Sarah?"

"Because," Emma said triumphantly, clicking on a photo album labelled 'Family History,' "of this."

The screen filled with an old black and white photo of a young woman holding a baby. The caption read: 'Me with my baby, 1962. Some losses you never forget.'

The young woman in the photo had Lisa's distinctive eyes.

"It's her," Rosie whispered. "It has to be."

Maria was already writing down the address of the retirement community. "How do we approach her? We can't just show up and say, 'Hello, we think you gave up a baby for adoption sixty years ago.'"

"We write to her first," Rosie decided. "Carefully, sensitively. Explain who Lisa is, what she's going through. Give Sarah the choice of whether to meet her."

"And if she says no?" Emma asked.

"Then at least we tried," Rosie said. "But I don't think she will. Look at that caption again. 'Some losses you never forget.' She's been thinking about Lisa all these years too."

"ARE YOU SURE ABOUT THIS?" Rosie asked, watching as Emma sealed the envelope containing their letter to Sarah. They'd spent ages crafting it, revising, arguing over every word, wanting to be both truthful and gentle.

"No," Emma admitted. "But I'm sure about Lisa. She deserves this chance."

"I included my mobile number," Maria said. "I thought it would be less overwhelming than having three contacts. And I'm usually the one with my phone actually turned on."

"Should we tell Lisa what we've done?" Rosie asked, the question that had been troubling her from the start.

"Not yet," Emma decided after a moment. "Not until we know if Sarah wants to meet her. No point getting her hopes up."

They stood together at the post-box, each touching the letter before Emma finally dropped it in. A small action, but one that might change their friend's life forever.

"Now we wait," Maria said.

THE CALL CAME JUST two days later. Maria was alone in the house, Lisa having gone to a hospital appointment with Rosie, and Emma out fetching groceries. Her phone rang with an unknown number, and something made her answer rather than letting it go to voicemail as she usually would.

"Hello?" A hesitant woman's voice came through. "Is this Maria Brydon? I received your letter about... about Lisa Mack."

Maria's heart leapt into her throat. "Yes, this is Maria. Thank you for calling."

There was a pause, filled with unspoken emotion. "Is it true? About Lisa's illness?"

"Yes," Maria said gently. "I'm afraid it is."

A soft sob came through the line. "All these years, I've thought about her. Wondered where she was, if she was happy. I tried to find her once, about twenty years ago, but the records were sealed, and I... I was afraid of disrupting her life."

"She'd love to meet you," Maria told her. "It's one of her deepest regrets, not finding you."

"I want to meet her," Sarah said with sudden conviction. "As soon as possible. I don't want to waste any more time."

"That's wonderful," Maria said, relief flooding through her. "I should warn you, though—Lisa doesn't know we've been looking for you. We wanted to be sure before getting her hopes up."

"I understand," Sarah replied. "Would it be easier if I came to you? I could take the train tomorrow."

"Tomorrow?" Maria hadn't expected things to move so quickly. "That would be... yes, that would be fine. I'll text you the address."

After ending the call, Maria sat in stunned silence for a moment before frantically texting Emma and Rosie: *She called. She's coming tomorrow. Lisa doesn't know yet. What do we do?*

Emma's reply came first: *We don't tell her. Let it be a surprise. Something good for once.*

Rosie's message came next: *No, she's ill. We can surprise her like that. We need to tell her first.*

THAT EVENING, as Lisa dozed on the sofa after dinner, the three women gathered in the kitchen under the pretence of washing up.

"She arrives at 10:30," Maria whispered. "I'll meet her at the station."

"Should we tell Lisa now, in the morning, or just let Sarah show up?" Rosie asked, concern creasing her brow. "We need to make a decision."

"Let's see how Lisa is feeling tomorrow," Emma suggested. "If she's having a good day, a surprise might be wonderful. If not..."

"Then we prepare her first," Maria finished. "We've come this far by being flexible."

"Whatever happens," Rosie said softly, "we've done what we set out to do. We've given her the chance she's always wanted."

IT WAS 8OAM. Half asleep, Rosie heard a sharp knock at the

door. She edged herself out of bed, extricating herself from the tangle of blankets, and made her way to answer it.

She opened the door to a woman she didn't recognise. The stranger, a well-dressed woman in her eighties, looked slightly nervous but determined.

"Hello," the woman said with a tentative smile. "You must be Lisa."

"No, I'm Rosie. Who are you?"

The woman took a deep breath. "I'm Sarah. Sarah Thompson —well, Wilson now. I'm..." her voice faltered slightly, "I'm Lisa's birth mother."

"What? I'm so sorry, we were supposed to pick you up at the station. Have we all overslept?"

"No. It's 8am," said Sarah. "I'm sorry. I couldn't wait any longer. I should have phoned, but my friend said he'd give me a lift and I grabbed the opportunity. Sorry."

"No, that's fine. Of course. Come in."

Behind them on the stairs there were footsteps. Rosie recognised them as Lisa's without even turning round.

"Lisa, someone's here to see you," she said. "This is Sarah. She's your birth mother."

THE MISSING PIECE ARRIVES

The world seemed to tilt on its axis. Lisa gripped the doorframe for support, her mind reeling. This was the moment she had both longed for and feared.

"Who's at the door?" Maria's sleepy voice called from inside. A moment later, she appeared, rubbing her eyes.

Rosie stood in silence, completely thrown by events, seemingly unable to communicate.

"Maria," Lisa turned to her friend, her voice barely above a whisper. "This woman says she's my birth mother."

"Oh my goodness. You're here," Maria said gently, stepping towards the door. "You were due to come later today. Lisa, we were going to tell you; we found her. We planned to have coffee in the garden this morning and tell you all about it."

"You found her." Lisa said, her eyes widening with wonder.

By now, the commotion had roused Emma, who appeared in the hallway looking sleepy but instantly alert at the sight of their visitor.

"Perhaps we should all go inside," Maria suggested warmly. "This isn't a conversation for the doorway."

As they made their way to the living room, Lisa's mind was spinning. Sarah—her birth mother—was here, in their home.

"We wanted to give you something special," Rosie explained softly. "After you mentioned your regret about never finding your birth mother..."

"We decided to try," Maria finished. "The three of us have been working on tracking her down."

Lisa looked between her friends, momentarily speechless, her eyes filling with tears. "I don't know what to say," she managed finally. "You did this for me?"

"We wanted it to be a wonderful surprise," Emma said, squeezing Lisa's hand. "Something good amidst everything else."

"And we weren't sure we'd succeed," Rosie explained. "We didn't want to raise your hopes only to disappoint you."

Sarah, who had been silent during this exchange, leaned forward slightly. "When I received Maria's letter explaining about your illness, I knew I had to come immediately. I've thought about you every day for sixty years, Lisa. Not knowing where you were, if you were happy... it's been my greatest sorrow that I couldn't find you when I looked."

Lisa turned to her birth mother, really looking at her for the first time. The resemblance was subtle but undeniable—the shape of the eyes, the way she held her hands. "You've been looking for me too?"

"Years ago," Sarah admitted. "But the records were sealed, and I... I was afraid of disrupting your life. I didn't know if you'd want to meet me."

"I've always wanted to meet you," Lisa whispered. "I had so many questions growing up. Even as an adult, I would look at strangers in the street and wonder if we were related."

Emma cleared her throat. "We'll give you two some privacy," she said, moving to stand.

"No," Lisa said firmly, reaching out to stop her. "Stay. All of you." Her eyes shone with gratitude as she looked at her friends.

"I want to share this moment with the people who made it possible. I still can't believe you did this for me."

"Well, Maria did most of the actual detective work," Emma admitted. "I just provided the nosiness and hounded people for information."

"And I made the lists," Rosie added with a smile.

Maria shrugged modestly. "It was a team effort. Although I must say, Emma's social media stalking skills are surprisingly advanced for someone who claims technology is 'the devil's plaything.'"

A laugh bubbled up from Lisa's chest, surprising even herself. "You three are extraordinary," she said, shaking her head in amazement. "Sneaking around, playing detective, writing letters to strangers..."

"Not just any stranger," Emma corrected. "Your mother. Who, by the way, has excellent taste in cardigans. I approve."

Sarah smiled gratefully at Emma before turning back to Lisa. "I know this is a shock. I understand if you need time to process. But I hoped... I hoped we might have a chance to know each other."

Lisa took a deep breath, feeling the supportive presence of her friends around her. "I'd like that very much," she said softly.

As the morning wore on, the initial surprise began to give way to genuine connection. Sarah shared stories of her life—her marriage to Robert, her career as a librarian, her two other children (Lisa's half-siblings) who lived in Australia. Lisa, in turn, told Sarah about her writing, her travels, the life she'd built.

The Sensational Sixty Squad, true to form, rallied around both women, filling in gaps in Lisa's stories, asking questions, and even managing to draw laughter from what could have been an overwhelming encounter.

Emma, in a moment of unexpected vulnerability, pulled Sarah aside. "Listen," she said, her voice uncharacteristically serious, "Lisa's been through a lot. We all have. If you're going to be in her life, you need to understand that you can't do anything to hurt her. I mean it. She's too vulnerable and her time is too precious for her to be messed around."

Sarah nodded, a look of respect in her eyes. "I understand. And I'm grateful that Lisa has such loyal friends. I hope, in time, I might earn your trust as well."

Later, as Sarah prepared to leave—plans made for another visit soon—Lisa pulled her three friends into a tight hug. "Thank you," she whispered, her voice thick with emotion. "You've given me something I never thought I'd have."

"We're rather good at meddling," Emma said with a wink. "It's one of our specialties."

After Sarah had gone, Lisa sought a moment of solitude in the garden. Rosie found her there, staring thoughtfully at the flowers.

"How are you feeling?" Rosie asked gently.

Lisa turned to her, tears glistening in her eyes. "Overwhelmed. Happy. Scared. I never thought I'd have this chance, Rosie. And now, with my health... I'm afraid of starting this relationship only to have it cut short."

Rosie pulled her friend into a tight hug. "Oh, Lisa. You can't think that way. Every moment we have is precious, whether it's a day or a decade."

"I know," Lisa whispered. "I know that."

THE FINAL PAGE TURNS

One morning in late October, Emma heard a cry from the room next to her. "I can't move. Everything's spinning. I don't know what's happened."

She jumped out of bed and ran in to talk to Lisa. Rosie and Maria heard the commotion and rushed to her room as well.

"I'm calling Dr. Sharma," Maria said quietly, already reaching for her phone.

"No hospitals," Lisa murmured without opening her eyes. "Please."

"Lisa, you need proper medical attention," Rosie insisted.

"Then have him come here," Lisa said. "I'm not spending any more time under fluorescent lights."

Dr. Sharma arrived within the hour, his normally composed face betraying concern as he examined Lisa. The women waited in the hallway, clutching mugs of tea gone cold.

"Her disease is progressing faster than we anticipated," he explained quietly. "I can adjust her medication to keep her comfortable, but..."

"But she doesn't have long," Emma finished, her voice barely above a whisper.

Dr. Sharma nodded solemnly. "She's adamant about staying home. I respect her wishes, but she'll need round-the-clock care."

"We'll manage," Maria said firmly.

"I'll also call Mike," Rosie added. "He's a GP, but having a doctor nearby would help, especially at night."

"A good idea," Dr. Sharma agreed. "I'll visit daily, and we'll arrange for a nursing team to come and administer intravenous drugs. If she sinks any further, we'll have to get her in though, we can't treat her here like we can treat her in hospital."

The next few days established a new rhythm in the household. The promised nursing team arrived each morning, efficiently checking Lisa's vitals and administering medication. Dr. Sharma visited in the afternoons, his quiet confidence reassuring them even as Lisa grew weaker. The women divided the remaining hours among themselves, making sure Lisa was never alone.

Rosie was returning from making a fresh pot of tea when she found Mike sitting beside Lisa's bed, his stethoscope around his neck, his expression more friend than physician. They'd grown closer over these difficult months, his initial awkwardness giving way to steady support that Rosie had come to rely on.

"How is she?" Rosie asked softly, setting the tea tray down beside the medication chart the nurses had left that morning.

Mike looked up, his tired eyes meeting hers. He took the cup she offered with a grateful nod.

"About the same," he said after taking a sip. "Dr. Sharma's medication is keeping her comfortable, but..." He didn't need to finish. They both knew there wasn't much time left.

A comfortable silence fell between them as they watched Lisa's gentle breathing. These quiet moments had become precious lately; little islands of calm in their sea of worry.

"Sarah called while you were downstairs," Mike said finally, changing the subject to something more hopeful. "Is she coming today?"

Rosie smiled, a rare moment of brightness in the sombre room. "Yes, this evening. She's been wonderful, you know. She and Lisa have formed such a beautiful connection. It's as if they're making up for lost time."

The days passed with a strange rhythm – mornings of hope when Lisa seemed stronger, afternoons of shared stories, evenings when her energy faded like the autumn light outside her window. The women had established a schedule, ensuring Lisa was never alone, while giving each other breaks to rest and gather their strength.

Sometimes they found themselves in the kitchen at odd hours, embracing as one or another broke down in silent tears, careful not to let Lisa hear. They were determined to be strong for her, though each carried the weight of impending loss like an invisible burden that bent their shoulders when Lisa couldn't see.

Dr. Sharma visited every day, making adjustments to Lisa's pain medication, his gentle manner offering as much comfort as his medical expertise. "She is not in pain," he assured them. "That's the most important thing now."

Later that afternoon, as Emma took her turn at Lisa's bedside, she found her friend awake and surprisingly alert.

"There you are," Lisa said, patting the space beside her. "I was beginning to think you'd abandoned me for that charming Gerald."

Emma snorted. "Please. He wears sandals with socks."

"A fashion crime indeed," Lisa agreed with a weak smile. "But he looks at you the way a starving man looks at a buffet."

"Now there's an appetising metaphor," Emma replied, though she couldn't hide her blush. "Anyway, we're not talking about my non-existent love life. We're focusing on you."

"That's precisely what I wanted to discuss," Lisa said,

suddenly serious. "I need you to get me something from my study. The bottom right drawer of my desk—there's a false bottom. You'll find some envelopes there."

Emma raised an eyebrow. "False bottom? Secret envelopes? Lisa Mack, you dark horse."

"Just get them for me," Lisa said, a trace of her old imperious tone returning. "And don't peek. They're not for you. Not yet."

Emma returned with the envelopes and placed them carefully in Lisa's hands, noting how thin her fingers had become, how the veins stood out blue against her pale skin. For a moment, Emma had to turn away, blinking rapidly to clear her vision.

On a quiet Sunday evening in early November, with the autumn sun setting, Lisa beckoned them all closer to her bed. Dr. Sharma had visited earlier, his face grave as he adjusted her medication and told her that she would be much better off in hospital. Lisa had point blank refused to go.

The envelopes lay on Lisa's bedside table. She'd refused to explain what they contained, saying only that they would understand "when the time was right."

Maria had brought fresh flowers, filling the room with the scent of lilies and roses. Rosie had arranged Lisa's pillows just so, ensuring she was comfortable. Mike waited quietly by the door, giving them privacy while remaining close enough to help if needed. And Emma had sneaked in a bottle of Lisa's favourite champagne, pouring tiny amounts into crystal glasses.

"To fabulous friends and a life well-lived," Lisa said, taking the smallest sip. "And to adventures yet to come—even the ones I won't be part of."

The women tried to match her smile, though each felt the effort like a physical pain. There was something about the way Lisa seemed both present and already halfway elsewhere that told them this was goodbye.

Lisa seemed to gather her remaining strength, as if for one

final important task. Her eyes, though sunken, held a remarkable clarity.

"Now then," she said, her voice barely above a whisper but still carrying that familiar note of authority. "I need to know you'll take care of each other. Emma, do try to learn the difference between a sauce and a soup. Maria, darling, stop worrying so much about everything - sometimes chaos is good for the soul. And Rosie...you and Mike should be together. Don't waste time when you find someone worth keeping."

She glanced meaningfully at Mike, who stood quietly in the doorway, his presence a steady comfort to them all over these difficult months.

"Lisa, please," Rosie began, but Lisa shook her head.

"I mean it. Promise me you'll keep having adventures. Keep making this house a home. Keep..." her voice faltered slightly, "keep remembering to laugh."

Maria took Lisa's hand, her usual composure cracking as tears slid silently down her cheeks. "We promise."

"And one more thing," Lisa continued, her voice growing fainter. "Those envelopes... there are photographs inside. Places that matter to me. Places you don't know about yet. I want you to scatter my ashes there. A final adventure for us all."

Lisa's eyes sparkled with a hint of her old mischief. "The envelopes will explain everything. Consider it my parting gift—the chance to discover who I really was. The parts of me I kept hidden."

"I always knew you were more mysterious than you let on," Emma said, trying to keep her voice light despite the tears that threatened to choke her. "Probably had a torrid affair with a foreign prince or something equally scandalous."

A ghost of a smile touched Lisa's lips. "Wait and see, darling. Wait and see."

As the light in the room deepened to amber, Lisa's breathing became more laboured. Mike stepped closer, checking her pulse with gentle fingers, his expression confirming what they already knew. The end was near.

"Read to me," Lisa whispered. "That poem I love."

Rosie reached for the book on the bedside table—a collection of verses they'd been exploring together. She found the marked page and began to read, her voice steady despite her tears:

"'Do not go gentle into that good night,
Old age should burn and rave at close of day;
Rage, rage against the dying of the light...'"

Emma moved to Lisa's other side, taking her hand—cool and papery thin, like autumn leaves—while Maria gently stroked her hair. The three of them formed a protective circle of love around their dying friend.

As Rosie's voice filled the room with Dylan Thomas's defiant words, something remarkable happened. The setting sun, which had been hidden behind clouds all day, suddenly broke through, flooding the room with extraordinary golden light. It illuminated Lisa's face, touching her dark hair with fire, lending her a momentary radiance that took their breath away.

Her eyes met each of theirs in turn, a lifetime of affection conveyed in those final glances. Then, with a soft sigh that seemed almost satisfied, like someone finishing a particularly good book, Lisa closed her eyes.

A profound peace seemed to settle over the room as her breathing slowed, then stopped altogether, a serene smile remaining on her face.

"Lisa?" Emma whispered, though she already knew.

Mike stepped forward, gently placing his fingers against Lisa's neck, then shook his head slightly. "She's gone," he said softly.

For a moment, no one moved. The warm radiance continued to fill the room, bathing them all in its glow, as if the universe itself was acknowledging Lisa's passage.

Then Emma made a small, broken sound—not quite a sob, but the noise of a heart cracking. Maria reached across Lisa's still form to grasp Emma's hand, forming an unbroken circle. Rosie lowered her face to Lisa's blanket, her shoulders shaking silently.

Outside, a gentle breeze stirred the autumn leaves, carrying them upward in a spiral dance against the golden sky. Inside, three women and a man who had become family through choice rather than blood began the first moments of a world without Lisa—holding each other, just as they had held her, until the very end.

"The doorbell rang softly an hour later. Mike went to answer it, returning with Sarah, who stopped in the doorway, understanding immediately what had happened. Her eyes filled with tears as she looked at the peaceful figure on the bed.

'I'm too late,' she whispered.

'No,' Rosie said gently, reaching out to her. 'You were part of her life at the end. That's what mattered to her.'

Sarah nodded, unable to speak. She moved quietly to the bedside, placing a small bouquet of wildflowers next to Lisa's hand. Though she had found her daughter too late for a lifetime of memories, she had been given enough time to know the extraordinary woman she had become—and the remarkable friends who had loved her so well."

NAVIGATING THE VOID

╾⚜╾

"The doorbell rang softly an hour later. Mike went to answer it, returning with Sarah, who stopped in the doorway, understanding immediately what had happened. Her eyes filled with tears as she looked at the peaceful figure on the bed.

'I'm too late,' she whispered.

'No,' Rosie said gently, reaching out to her. 'You were part of her life at the end. That's what mattered to her.'

Sarah nodded, unable to speak. She moved quietly to the bedside, placing a small bouquet of wildflowers next to Lisa's hand. Though she had found her daughter too late for a lifetime of memories, she had been given enough time to know the extraordinary woman she had become—and the remarkable friends who had loved her so well."

"The doorbell rang softly an hour later. Mike went to answer it, returning with Sarah, who stopped in the doorway, understanding immediately what had happened. Her eyes filled with tears as she looked at the peaceful figure on the bed.

'I'm too late,' she whispered.

'No,' Rosie said gently, reaching out to her. 'You were part of her life at the end. That's what mattered to her.'

Sarah nodded, unable to speak. She moved quietly to the bedside, placing a small bouquet of wildflowers next to Lisa's hand. Though she had found her daughter too late for a lifetime of memories, she had been given enough time to know the extraordinary woman she had become—and the remarkable friends who had loved her so well."

"The doorbell rang softly an hour later. Mike went to answer it, returning with Sarah, who stopped in the doorway, understanding immediately what had happened. Her eyes filled with tears as she looked at the peaceful figure on the bed.

'I'm too late,' she whispered.

'No,' Rosie said gently, reaching out to her. 'You were part of her life at the end. That's what mattered to her.'

Sarah nodded, unable to speak. She moved quietly to the bedside, placing a small bouquet of wildflowers next to Lisa's hand. Though she had found her daughter too late for a lifetime of memories, she had been given enough time to know the extraordinary woman she had become—and the remarkable friends who had loved her so well."

"The doorbell rang softly an hour later. Mike went to answer it, returning with Sarah, who stopped in the doorway, understanding immediately what had happened. Her eyes filled with tears as she looked at the peaceful figure on the bed.

'I'm too late,' she whispered.

'No,' Rosie said gently, reaching out to her. 'You were part of her life at the end. That's what mattered to her.'

Sarah nodded, unable to speak. She moved quietly to the bedside, placing a small bouquet of wildflowers next to Lisa's hand. Though she had found her daughter too late for a lifetime of memories, she had been given enough time to know the extraordinary woman she had become—and the remarkable friends who had loved her so well.

For a long moment, none of them moved. The golden light continued to bathe the room, as if reluctant to leave along with Lisa's spirit. Then Maria began to weep, quiet dignified tears that seemed to break the spell holding them all in place.

Emma reached out and gently closed Lisa's eyes, her own face wet with tears she hadn't realised she was shedding. "Safe travels, old girl," she whispered. "Give 'em hell wherever you're going."

Rosie sat frozen, still holding Lisa's hand, unable or unwilling to let go. Mike moved behind her, placing his hands gently on her shoulders in silent support.

"She looks peaceful," Maria said finally, her voice thick with emotion. "Almost like she's just sleeping."

"That's what people always say, isn't it?" Emma replied, a hint of her usual sharpness returning despite her tears. "But she's not sleeping. She's gone. Our Lisa is gone."

The reality of those words hung in the air, undeniable and crushing. The room that had been filled with Lisa's vibrant presence for so many months now contained only her empty shell, beautiful and serene but unmistakably abandoned.

That night, after the necessary calls had been made and Lisa's body taken away, the house fell into an eerie quiet. The three remaining women moved like ghosts themselves, unable to settle, unable to name the loss that seemed to echo through every room.

Rosie found herself standing in the doorway of Lisa's bedroom at midnight, staring at the empty bed still bearing the impression of her friend's body. The sheets had been changed, the medical equipment removed, but Lisa's perfume lingered in the air – that distinctive blend of sandalwood and jasmine that had always announced her presence.

"I can't believe she's really gone," Rosie whispered to the empty room.

From behind her, Mike's voice came softly. "I thought I

might find you here." He'd stayed, understanding instinctively that they would need him. He wrapped a gentle arm around Rosie's shoulders. "She was extraordinary."

"She was," Rosie agreed, leaning into his solid presence. "And now there's just this... hole where she should be."

Down the hall, Emma sat on her bed, a glass of Lisa's favourite scotch in her hand. She hadn't bothered with proper glassware – Lisa would have been appalled – but somehow drinking straight from the bottle felt like too much of a cliché, even in grief.

"To you, you magnificent, maddening woman," she whispered, raising the glass to the photograph of Lisa on her nightstand. "If there's any justice in the universe, you're already reorganising heaven and criticising the angels' fashion choices."

In her meticulously organised room, Maria sat surrounded by paper and coloured pens, creating a detailed timeline of Lisa's care, her treatments, her good days and bad. It was her way of imposing order on the chaos of loss, of making sense of the senseless. But when she reached the final entry – "November 5th, 7:42 pm: Lisa departed" – her careful handwriting dissolved into an uncharacteristic scrawl as tears blurred her vision.

The morning after Lisa's death brought reality crashing in. They found themselves moving through the immediate aftermath in a sort of daze, though each tried to honour Lisa's wishes for no excessive moping. Emma handled the funeral arrangements with unexpected efficiency, while Rosie dealt with official paperwork. Maria, to everyone's surprise, took charge of Lisa's extensive wardrobe, cataloguing each piece with the same attention to detail her friend had always shown.

"I found this," Maria said on the second morning, holding up a leather-bound ledger. "It's her will. She's updated it recently—everything's arranged down to the smallest detail."

"That sounds like Lisa," Rosie said, accepting the document with trembling hands.

Inside, they found everything meticulously organised—from Lisa's financial affairs to specific bequests for each of them. Emma was to receive the vintage champagne collection and first choice of jewellery. Maria inherited the designer suits that had always looked better on her tall frame. Rosie was given the first editions and art collection. And to all of them jointly, the mysterious envelopes, with explicit instructions not to open them until after the funeral.

"She thought of everything," Emma said, equal parts impressed and heartbroken.

"Not quite everything," Maria replied softly, holding up a sealed letter addressed to 'My Birth Mother.' "She never finished this."

Rosie took the letter, her throat tight with emotion. "We'll make sure Sarah gets it. Lisa would want that."

Mike arrived then, having left briefly to arrange for Lisa's body to be taken to the funeral home she'd specified in her will. "How are you all holding up?" he asked, his eyes particularly concerned as they rested on Rosie.

"We're following Lisa's instructions," she replied, gesturing to the will. "No moping allowed."

"Though some discreet crying in the bathroom is permitted," Emma added, attempting a smile that didn't quite reach her eyes.

Mike nodded, understanding their need to maintain some semblance of normalcy. "I've spoken with the funeral director. Everything's arranged as Lisa wanted."

"Thank you," Rosie said, reaching for his hand. "For everything. These past months... I don't know what we would have done without you."

"I'm not going anywhere," he replied, the simple promise carrying weight far beyond the immediate situation.

Over the next four days, as funeral arrangements took shape, the women found comfort in small rituals. Each morning, they met in the kitchen as they always had, though the fourth chair remained painfully empty. Each evening, they shared a bottle from Lisa's collection, toasting her memory with stories that gradually brought more laughter than tears.

"The blue Chanel suits you," Emma said softly on the fifth day, finding Maria in Lisa's room, running her hands over the familiar fabrics. "She'd like that."

"I keep expecting to hear her voice," Maria admitted. "Telling me I'm folding things wrong."

"Or critiquing my soup-making technique," Emma added with a sad smile.

"Or reminding me that colour-coding isn't actually a personality trait," Maria said, a tear slipping down her cheek despite her smile.

Rosie stood in the doorway, watching her friends find comfort in memories and Lisa's beautiful things. "She left such detailed instructions for everything," she said. "Even her funeral is planned down to the last champagne cork."

"Trust Lisa to micromanage her own funeral," Emma replied, but the familiar snark held a new note of fondness and grief.

"Should we look at the photographs?" Maria asked hesitantly, gesturing to the still-sealed envelopes on Lisa's desk. "She said to wait until after the funeral, but—"

"We'll wait," Rosie interrupted gently. "She had her reasons for the timing. Let's honour that, at least."

The day before the funeral, a package arrived from Lisa's dressmaker – three outfits in vibrant colours, perfectly tailored to each woman's measurements. A note in Lisa's handwriting read simply: "For my send-off. No black allowed, remember?"

In the evening, they gathered in the kitchen, their usual meeting place, and opened a bottle from Lisa's collection.

"To Lisa," Emma said, raising her glass. "Who taught us how to live—and how to say goodbye."

"To Lisa," they echoed, the familiar ritual now carrying new weight and meaning.

As they sipped the expensive wine, Rosie couldn't help but feel that something fundamental had shifted in their shared home. It wasn't just Lisa's absence—though that was a gaping hole in the fabric of their lives. It was the knowledge that they were changed, irrevocably, by loving and losing her.

"We should get some rest," Mike suggested gently. "Tomorrow will be... challenging."

They nodded, knowing he was right. The funeral loomed ahead of them—a final public farewell to their beloved friend. After that would come the mystery of the photographs and whatever posthumous adventure Lisa had planned for them.

As they headed upstairs, each to her own room, Rosie paused at Lisa's door, unable to resist one final look. In the moonlight streaming through the window, she could almost imagine her friend still there, elegant in silk pyjamas, reading glasses perched on her nose as she worked on her latest writing project.

"Goodnight, Lisa," she whispered. "Save a place for us, won't you?"

A COLOURFUL FAREWELL

After days of typical English drizzle, the sky had cleared overnight, revealing a beautiful pale blue sky that seemed to mock the occasion with its perfection. The sort of day Lisa would have claimed she'd arranged personally.

Rosie, Emma and Maria gathered in the kitchen, each dressed in the colourful attire Lisa had specifically requested. No black allowed—that had been her first and most emphatic funeral rule.

Rosie wore a sapphire blue dress that Lisa had always admired, claiming it brought out her eyes. Maria had selected a deep emerald suit—one of Lisa's own that their friend often insisted would look better on Maria's taller frame. Emma had chosen a patterned jumpsuit in shades of fuchsia and orange that had drawn a shocked laugh from the others when she'd appeared downstairs.

"What?" she'd asked innocently. "Lisa said no black and 'wear something fabulous.' If this isn't fabulous, I don't know what is."

"It's certainly... eye-catching," Maria conceded, adjusting her own perfect tailoring.

"Lisa would have had opinions," Rosie said with a sad smile.

"Loud ones," Emma agreed fondly. "She'd have critiqued the fabric choice while simultaneously admiring my boldness."

The doorbell chimed, its cheerful tone at odds with the day's purpose.

"That'll be Mike," Rosie said, smoothing her dress and checking her reflection one last time in the hallway mirror.

But when she opened the door, it was Julie who stood on the threshold, her silver-streaked dark hair pulled into an artful knot, wearing a handmade kaftan in swirls of purple and teal that only she could carry off. Paintbrush-shaped earrings dangled from her ears, catching the morning light.

"Oh, darling," Julie said, enveloping Rosie in a hug that smelled of oil paints and expensive sandalwood perfume. "What a hideous day to be so beautiful."

"Julie!" Rosie stepped back, genuinely pleased. "I thought you were in Norfolk this week."

"As if I'd miss this." Julie handed over a small canvas wrapped in tissue paper. "For later. A little remembrance piece. Nothing maudlin—Lisa would have hated that."

Before Rosie could respond, a sleek silver Audi pulled up behind Julie's tatty old Citroën. Catherine emerged from the passenger side, elegant in a structured dress of coral silk. Even at this distance, Rosie could see that her makeup was flawless, her blonde bob freshly trimmed.

The driver's door opened, and a tall man with the confident bearing of someone used to commanding rooms stepped out.

"Oh God," Emma murmured, appearing at Rosie's elbow. "She's brought Richard."

"Be nice," Rosie hissed. "It's a funeral."

"Lisa would have expected us to maintain standards," Emma retorted. "Especially about him."

Richard strode ahead of Catherine, hand extended as if arriving at a business meeting rather than a funeral. "Ladies," he greeted them with practised charm. "Terrible day. Simply terrible. I've been telling Catherine she should have checked in on poor Lisa more often."

Catherine winced visibly, her composure slipping for just a moment before her social mask clicked back into place. "Richard insisted on driving me," she explained, the apology clear in her eyes. "I hope that's alright."

"Of course it is," Rosie assured her, stepping forward to embrace her friend. She whispered in Catherine's ear, "Though Lisa would have had choice words about his attendance."

Catherine's soft laugh held a hint of genuine relief. "She absolutely would have."

"Actually," Richard announced, checking his watch with exaggerated care, "I have a conference call in twenty minutes. I'll just drop Catherine off with you ladies, shall I? Pick her up after? Text me when it's over, darling."

Before anyone could respond, he had kissed Catherine's cheek with mechanical precision and was sliding back into his car.

"Well," Emma said into the awkward silence that followed his departure, "at least that's one person Lisa won't have to haunt for wearing the wrong outfit."

Catherine's shoulders relaxed visibly as the Audi disappeared down the road. "I'm sorry about that. He insisted..."

"Don't apologise," Julie said, linking arms with her. "That man has been 'insisting' since 1982. We're just glad you're here."

"And Richard-free," Emma added.

The tension broken, they moved into the hallway just as Mike arrived, handsome in a dark blue suit brightened by a vibrant pocket square—his own nod to Lisa's instructions.

"Ladies," he greeted them with gentle warmth, his eyes finding Rosie's immediately. "You all look wonderful. Very Lisa-approved."

"Let's hope so," Rosie replied, gathering her purse. "She was very specific about the dress code. I wouldn't put it past her to haunt anyone who showed up in funeral black."

"I mentioned that to Tom last night," Julie said, adjusting her dramatic sleeve. "When he called to ask if I was actually wearing 'circus colours' to a funeral."

A shadow crossed her expressive face. "He's taking Janine to Barcelona next week. Her first time there. He knows how I've always wanted to see the Gaudi buildings."

Emma squeezed Julie's arm. "His loss. When this is over, we'll plan a proper Barcelona trip. Just us. No husbands, ex or otherwise."

Julie's smile didn't quite reach her eyes. "That would be lovely. Though I'd settle for a guest room at your place at this point. The cottage feels so empty now." She forced a bright laugh. "Listen to me, making today about my troubles! Lisa would have told me to save the self-pity for my art."

"She would have offered you her room in a heartbeat, too," Maria said quietly. "You know that."

Julie nodded, blinking rapidly. "I know. I was going to move in with you girls when you found that place in Esher but kept thinking Tom would come back. Silly, after three years. But now, seeing him plan trips with her... I've wasted so much time waiting."

Catherine touched her shoulder in silent understanding.

They made one final check of the house—lights off, doors locked, Lisa's favourite flowers arranged in vases throughout the rooms. It felt important somehow, to leave everything perfect, as if she might return at any moment to inspect their efforts.

As they gathered outside, arranging themselves between Mike's sensible Volvo and Julie's artistic mess of a vehicle, Catherine hesitated. "Would you mind if I ride with you? I'm not quite up to facing Richard immediately after the service."

"Of course," Rosie said. "There's plenty of room."

"You could make that arrangement permanent, you know," Emma added with her characteristic directness as they settled into the cars. "Lisa always said you needed to boot that man properly out of your life."

"Emma!" Maria admonished from the front seat. "Today is hardly the time."

"On the contrary," Emma retorted. "Today is exactly the time. If Lisa's death teaches us anything, it's that time is short and we shouldn't waste time on people who diminish us."

Catherine stared out the window for a long moment before responding. "She did say that, didn't she? The last time we had lunch. 'Catherine, darling, life's too short to spend it managing a man who can't manage himself.'" Her impression of Lisa's crisp diction was so perfect that laughter caught them all by surprise.

As the cars pulled away from the house, the six of them—four housemates and two friends drawn into their orbit by Lisa's magnetic presence—faced the hard task ahead. But somehow, the burden felt lighter shared between them.

THE CHAPEL WAS ALREADY FILLING when they arrived. Lisa might have been private about her illness, but news of her passing had travelled quickly through her wide network of friends, colleagues, and admirers. Literary figures mingled with politicians, fashion designers chatted with university professors, all united in their affection for the remarkable woman they'd come to honour.

"I had no idea she knew so many people," Rosie murmured, overwhelmed by the turnout.

"Lisa collected interesting people the way some collect stamps," Emma replied. "And she never forgot anyone who mattered to her."

Julie scanned the crowd with an artist's eye for detail. "Look at those colours! She'd be thrilled. Not a funeral director's nightmare in sight."

Indeed, the congregation bloomed with colour—jewel tones, pastels, vibrant prints, and not a sombre black suit to be seen. The effect was of a garden in full bloom rather than a funeral.

The scent of lilies filled the chapel, their sweet fragrance almost overwhelming in the enclosed space. Soft classical music —Lisa's beloved Mozart—played in the background as people found their seats. The casket at the front was closed, draped not with flowers but with a vintage Hermès scarf in vibrant shades of turquoise and coral—another of Lisa's specific requests.

Julie reached into her enormous tapestry bag and produced a small sketch pad and pencil.

"Really, Jules?" Catherine whispered, though without censure.

"She'd expect me to capture the moment," Julie replied, her pencil already moving across the paper. "Besides, it helps me... process."

Catherine nodded, understanding. They each had their ways of coping.

The service was elegant without being stuffy, meaningful without being maudlin. There were readings from her favourite books, pieces of classical music she had loved, and not a single religious platitude to be found. Sarah, Lisa's birth mother, sat in the front row, her face a study in complex grief—the sorrow of losing a daughter she had only just found.

Then it was Emma's turn to speak. She approached the podium with uncharacteristic nervousness, her colourful outfit a bright splash against the chapel's muted tones. For a moment, she simply stood there, looking out at the sea of faces—some familiar, many not—all waiting to hear her words about their beloved friend.

"Lisa Mack was not a perfect woman," Emma began, her voice steadier than she'd expected. "She could be impossibly demanding, terrifyingly blunt, and God help anyone who crossed her before she'd had her morning coffee."

Appreciative chuckles rippled through the audience.

"But she was perfect in all the ways that truly mattered," Emma continued. "Perfect in her loyalty, her fierce intelligence, her unfailing ability to tell you exactly what you needed to hear —whether you wanted to hear it or not."

She spoke of Lisa's professional brilliance—how she had elevated ghost writing to an art form, giving voice to those who had stories to tell but lacked her gift with words. She shared anecdotes of their adventures together—the midnight skinny dipping expedition that had nearly resulted in hypothermia and arrest, the salsa dancing competition where Lisa had charmed the judges despite stepping on her partner's toes, the skydiving adventure that had left them all exhilarated and terrified in equal measure.

"Then we all moved in together and called ourselves the Sensational Sixties Squad," Emma said, her voice growing thick with emotion despite her best efforts. "Four women of a certain age who refused to go quietly into that good night. And no one raged against the dying of the light more brilliantly than Lisa."

From her seat in the front row, Rosie felt the dual weight of grief and pride—sorrow at Lisa's absence, pride in Emma's perfect capturing of their friend's spirit. Beside her, Maria clutched a handkerchief embroidered with Lisa's initials, a small treasure she'd found while organising the wardrobe.

In the row behind, Julie's pencil moved steadily across her pad, capturing the scene in swift, sure strokes—Emma's defiant posture at the podium, the sea of colourful mourners, the sunlight streaming through the windows. Catherine sat with perfect posture, eyes fixed forward, one hand occasionally rising to brush away tears with practiced discretion.

Emma paused, looking down at her notes, then deliberately set them aside. "Lisa once told me," she continued, her voice steady despite her tears, "that life was too short for sensible shoes and small dreams. She lived that philosophy every day and expected no less from those around her."

She looked out at the gathered mourners, many now openly weeping despite Lisa's strict "no misery" policy. "So here's what Lisa would want me to tell you today: Don't waste time. Don't postpone joy. Don't save your good china or your expensive perfume for 'someday.' Live now, love fiercely, laugh often, and always—**always**—wear the outrageous outfit."

As Emma returned to her seat, a spontaneous applause broke out—an unusual sound in a chapel but somehow perfectly appropriate for Lisa's final farewell.

Rosie squeezed her hand. "That was beautiful," she whispered. "She would have loved it."

"Not too sappy?" Emma asked anxiously.

"Just sappy enough," Rosie assured her with a watery smile.

The service continued with more music, more readings, more celebrations of a life well-lived. A former Home Secretary stood to speak, sharing how Lisa had transformed his political memoirs from "dry recitation to something people might actually want to read."

And then, as the final notes of Lisa's favourite aria faded away, something remarkable happened: a perfect rainbow arched over the chapel, its colours brilliant against the autumn sky.

The stained-glass windows, ordinary until that moment, suddenly blazed with colour as the sun hit them at precisely the right angle. A cascade of jewel-toned light spilled across the gathering, bathing everyone in shades of ruby, sapphire, emerald, and amethyst. The effect was so stunning that a collective gasp went up from the mourners.

It was the kind of theatrical gesture that Lisa herself might have arranged—dramatic, beautiful, and timed perfectly for maximum impact.

"She's making an entrance at her own funeral," Emma whispered, a half-laugh, half-sob catching in her throat. "Typical Lisa."

Julie's pencil flew across the page, trying to capture the impossible play of light before it faded.

"Some things can't be sketched, only remembered," Catherine said softly, placing a hand on Julie's arm.

Julie nodded, setting down her pad. "She always did know how to steal the show."

AFTER THE SERVICE came the wake, held in the garden of a nearby hotel. The unseasonable warmth allowed for an outdoor gathering, with the late autumn roses still blooming as if in tribute. True to Lisa's instructions, champagne flowed freely, delicate canapés circulated on silver trays, and music played in the background—the same quartet that had performed in their living room during the cheese tasting adventure. The mood was one of celebration rather than mourning—exactly as Lisa had demanded.

Julie had set up an impromptu display of her quick sketches from the service, propped against a stone wall. Mourners gathered around them, finding comfort in her artistic interpretation of their shared grief.

"These are extraordinary, Jules," Rosie said, studying a swift impression of the rainbow light flooding the chapel. "You've captured it perfectly."

"Art therapy," Julie replied with a self-deprecating shrug. "Cheaper than a shrink."

"You should exhibit these," Catherine suggested, joining them with three champagne flutes balanced expertly in her hands.

Julie shook her head. "They're not for selling. They're for

remembering." She accepted a glass from Catherine, raising it slightly. "To Lisa, who'd be critiquing my line work even now."

"With devastating accuracy," Catherine agreed with a fond smile.

"But always constructively," Rosie added.

They sipped in companionable silence until Julie spoke again, her voice barely audible over the quartet. "Tom's selling our cottage." She stared into her champagne. "I didn't want to tell you earlier, but he's moving in with Janine permanently. Wants to 'settle things.'"

"Oh, Jules," Catherine squeezed her arm.

"It's fine," Julie said with forced brightness. "It's been three years. I should have faced reality sooner. Lisa kept telling me not to put my life on hold for him." She blinked rapidly. "I should have listened."

"It's never too late to start listening," Rosie said gently. "The house has felt so empty since..." She didn't need to finish the thought.

Julie looked between them, comprehension dawning. "Are you suggesting...?"

"Lisa's room," Rosie confirmed. "Not right away, of course. But eventually, when we're all ready."

"We'd have to set up a proper studio space for you," Catherine mused, warming to the idea. "The conservatory gets beautiful northern light."

"You too?" Julie asked, eyebrows raised.

Catherine flushed slightly. "Well, I... Richard thinks I should downsize now the children have moved out. He's been pushing me to sell the house."

"Of course he has," Emma interjected, appearing with a fresh bottle of champagne. "Prime real estate he wants a cut of, I'm sure."

"Emma," Rosie warned.

"No, she's right," Catherine said with surprising firmness.

"It's exactly what he's doing. And I'm tired of it. Tired of managing his expectations and demands even though we've been divorced for years."

"So what are you saying?" Julie asked.

"I'm saying Lisa was right. About all of it." Catherine's perfectly manicured hand tightened around her glass. "Life's too short to spend it trying to please people who drain you."

"Lisa would drink to that," Emma declared, topping up their glasses. "So should we."

The reception continued well into the evening. As the crowd began to thin, Mike approached Rosie, two champagne flutes in hand.

"How are you holding up?" he asked gently, passing her a glass.

"Better than I expected," she admitted. "It helps, somehow, knowing exactly what she wanted. It's like she's still directing us all from beyond."

"She was a remarkable woman," Mike said. "I wish I'd known her for longer."

"So do I," Rosie replied, leaning slightly against his solid warmth. "But I'm grateful you were there at the end. For her, and for me."

His arm slipped around her waist, a gesture of comfort that felt both new and familiar.

Across the garden, Julie and Catherine sat together beneath a rose arbour, their heads bent in conversation, occasional laughter drifting over on the evening breeze. Something about their posture—relaxed, intimate, conspiratorial—reminded Rosie of the early days at Lavender Lane, when four strangers were becoming family.

As the last of the guests departed, Rosie, Emma, Maria, Mike, Julie, and Catherine found themselves standing alone in the garden, glasses in hand, looking up at the first stars appearing in the deepening blue sky. The air had cooled, carrying the scent of the garden roses.

"To Lisa," Rosie said softly. "Who taught us how to live, right up until the end."

"To Lisa," the others echoed, the familiar toast now carrying new weight and meaning. The glasses clinked together, the sound like a small crystal bell in the quiet garden.

Julie looked at the circle of friends around her. "You know, this feels like the beginning of something, doesn't it? Even in the midst of an ending."

As they gathered their belongings to leave, Catherine paused, her phone in hand. "Richard's texted three times asking when I'll be ready to be collected." She stared at the screen for a long moment, then deliberately tucked the phone into her bag without responding. "I think I'll go back with you, Julie, if that's alright."

"More than alright," Julie said warmly. "We can plan our Barcelona trip on the way."

The six of them walked together toward the exit, their colourful outfits a final tribute to the woman who had brought them together.

In the fading light, Rosie could almost hear Lisa's voice: "Well, don't just stand there looking gorgeous, darlings. The next chapter won't write itself."

CORNWALL CALLING

A month after the funeral, they gathered in the kitchen, staring at the urn that contained the earthly remains of their beloved friend. Beside it lay three sealed envelopes, each bearing a different number written in Lisa's flowing script.

"I suppose it's time," Rosie said softly, reaching for the envelope marked "1".

They had postponed opening the envelopes until now, each woman privately dreading the finality of what would follow. But Lisa's instructions had been clear—this was to be their final adventure together, and she wouldn't want them delaying.

November had melted into December, bringing shorter days and a chill that seemed to seep into their bones. The house felt different now; quieter in some ways yet still filled with Lisa's presence. They had gradually settled into new routines, finding comfort in shared meals and quiet evenings, but they avoided talk of the future beyond their immediate plans.

The sealed envelopes had waited patiently on the mantelpiece, a daily reminder of unfinished business. Now, with Christmas decorations in neighbours' windows, they had finally felt ready to take this next step in their grieving process.

Emma poured four glasses of Lisa's favourite champagne. "She'd approve of this," she said, handing them around, and leaving one next to Lisa's place. "Nothing marks the beginning of an adventure better than good champagne at ten in the morning."

Maria cleared her throat. "Should we read it aloud, or...?"

"Together," Rosie decided. "That's how Lisa would want it."

With trembling fingers, she broke the seal and extracted a photograph and a folded sheet of Lisa's personal stationery. The photograph showed a small, picturesque fishing village, its harbour filled with colourful boats, with whitewashed cottages climbing up steep hillsides.

"Port Isaac," Maria identified immediately. "North Cornwall coast."

"How do you know that?" Emma asked, impressed despite herself.

"I've been there," Maria replied simply. "Family holiday, years ago. It's beautiful. I didn't know that Lisa had any connection to it though"

Rosie unfolded the letter and began to read aloud:

My darlings,

If you're reading this, then I've finally managed the one thing I could never accomplish in life—leaving you all speechless. (Emma, close your mouth, darling. It's not an attractive look.)

Emma snorted, instinctively snapping her mouth shut.

Port Isaac was where I spent the summer of my nineteenth year, working as a waitress and having my heart thoroughly broken by a local fisherman's son. James Porter was his name—tall, broad-shouldered, with eyes the colour of the Atlantic after a storm. He was my first great love, and the first to teach me that love, no matter how passionate, isn't always enough.

What you don't know—what I've never told anyone—is that I returned there every year on the anniversary of our parting. Not out of lingering attachment, but to remind myself of the girl I once was: fearless, passionate, willing to risk everything for love.

I want a quarter of my ashes scattered from the harbour wall at sunrise. It's quiet then, magical. The fishermen will be heading out, the village still sleeping. There's a particular spot—the northernmost point where the wall curves slightly. I've marked it on the photograph: you'll know it when you see it.

This is where I learned that endings can also be beginnings. That heartbreak doesn't kill you but makes you both stronger and more tender. A lesson I've carried throughout my life.

Now go have a cream tea at Mrs. Baxter's Tea Room (if it's still there—ask for the back table with the harbour view), and toast James Porter, wherever he may be. Without him, I might never have learned the resilience that carried me through life—and through my final days with all of you.

With all my love (and just a touch of my usual bossiness), Lisa x

P.S. Emma, do NOT flirt with the local fishermen. They haven't evolved since the 1970s.

For a while, none of them spoke. The revelation of this unknown chapter of Lisa's life—this yearly pilgrimage she'd never mentioned—left them speechless.

"I had no idea," Rosie said finally. "All those weekend trips she claimed were for research..."

"It's quite romantic, isn't it?" Maria mused, her practical nature momentarily giving way to sentimentality. "Returning to the place where her heart was first broken, year after year."

"Not romantic," Emma corrected. "Deliberate. Lisa wasn't dwelling on heartbreak; she was celebrating her own strength. That's the point."

Rosie nodded slowly. "You're right. This wasn't about James Porter. It was about Lisa Mack reminding herself of who she was at her core."

They fell silent again, each contemplating this new understanding of their friend. Lisa, who had always seemed so self-assured, so completely formed, had deliberately maintained this connection to her younger self.

"Well," Emma said briskly, raising her glass, "when do we leave for Cornwall?"

Emma circled January 8th on the kitchen calendar with a red marker. "Three weeks. That gives us time to get through Christmas without..." Her voice faltered.

"Without it being about grief," Maria finished, closing the laptop where she'd been researching routes. "Lisa would hate us moping through the holidays on her account."

"So it's settled," Rosie said, running her finger along the coastal route on the map spread across the table. "We drive." She glanced at the small silver container sitting on the mantelpiece, catching the winter light. "It feels more... private that way."

"Plus, we can stop whenever we want," Emma added. "No schedules, no rushing. Just us and the open road."

"And Lisa," Maria said softly, folding the map with practiced precision.

FROST SPARKLED on the windshield as they loaded the car at dawn three weeks later. Their breath formed small clouds in the January air. Emma scraped the ice with vigorous strokes while Maria arranged a thermos of coffee, three travel mugs, and a bag of pastries in the front seat.

"Keys!" Emma called, holding out her hand as Rosie approached from the house.

Rosie hesitated. "Are you sure you want to drive the whole way? It's nearly six hours."

"Absolutely," Emma replied, jingling her fingers impatiently. "I've seen how you drive. Like an octogenarian with glaucoma."

"I'm careful," Rosie protested.

"You're funereal," Emma countered. "And this trip isn't a funeral. It's an adventure."

Rosie surrendered the keys, then paused at the passenger door. "Wait. I almost forgot." She hurried back to the house, returning moments later with her handbag clutched close to her chest. She slid into the back seat, opening her bag just enough for them to glimpse the silver container nestled among tissues.

Emma met her eyes in the rearview mirror and nodded once. No words needed.

"RECALCULATING," chirped the GPS for the third time in twenty minutes.

Maria slapped it silent and unfurled her paper map across her knees. "Technology," she muttered, tracing their route with her finger. "Take the next left. The *actual* left, not whatever this electronic menace suggests."

The car rounded a bend, revealing a panorama of coastline—jagged cliffs dropping to a winter sea that shifted between slate and silver under the changing sky.

"Oh," Maria breathed.

Emma slowed the car, allowing them to absorb the view. "She would have had something clever to say about this," she said after a moment. "Something about nature's drama queen tendencies."

Rosie leaned forward between the seats. "I can almost hear her voice."

"JESUS CHRIST ON A POGO STICK!" Emma wrenched the steering wheel as the stone wall scraped perilously close to the passenger side. The lane had narrowed to barely the width of the car, with ancient Cornish walls pressing in on both sides.

"Perhaps you should slow down?" Maria suggested, white-knuckled fingers gripping the door handle.

"Any slower and we'll be going backward," Emma retorted,

hunching forward over the wheel. "This isn't a road. It's a medieval torture device disguised as infrastructure."

"Lisa would be loving this," Rosie said from the back seat, a wistful smile playing at her lips.

"She'd be critiquing my every move," Emma grunted, navigating another hairpin turn.

"No," Rosie shook her head. "She'd be leaning forward, just like this—" she demonstrated, pressing her arms against the front seats, "—with that half-smile she got whenever life got unpredictable. She thrived on moments like this."

The car fell silent except for the crunch of tyres on gravel and the distant sound of gulls.

"Take the next right," Maria said finally, her voice softer. "We're almost there."

THE VILLAGE APPEARED before them like an illustration from a storybook—whitewashed cottages tumbling down to a natural harbour, fishing boats nestled together for protection from the winter seas. The afternoon light was already fading, lending everything a golden-blue quality.

Emma parked on the village outskirts. No cars were allowed down the precipitous main street that led to the harbour. They gathered their overnight bags, Rosie clutching her handbag a little tighter than the others.

The Sea Breeze B&B was a three-story cottage with window boxes still sporting hardy winter pansies. A brass bell tinkled as they pushed open the door, releasing the scent of cinnamon and furniture polish.

Mrs. Trewin emerged from the back room, wiping her hands on a flowered apron. Sharp eyes assessed them from behind tortoiseshell glasses.

"You'll be the London ladies, then?" She consulted a leather-bound reservation book. "Three nights, is it?"

"Yes," Maria confirmed. "We requested rooms overlooking the harbour, if possible."

Mrs. Trewin's eyebrows rose a fraction. "Odd choice for January. The fishing boats start before dawn—make a right racket with their engines."

Emma leaned on the reception desk, her smile disarming. "That's rather the point. We're here for the authentic experience."

Mrs. Trewin's gaze flickered between the three women.

"Someone special bring you here, did they?" she asked, her tone gentler.

Rosie nodded, not trusting herself to speak.

Mrs. Trewin handed over three old-fashioned keys with heavy brass fobs. "Rooms 3, 4, and 5. Best views in the house."

THE EVENING AIR bit at their cheeks as they descended the steep cobbled street toward the harbour. Their footsteps echoed between silent cottages, most still decorated with Christmas lights that glowed softly in the gathering dusk.

The harbour lay before them, fishing boats bobbing gently at their moorings. The tide was high, water slapping rhythmically against the stone wall. Rosie pulled Lisa's letter from her pocket, the paper already soft from frequent handling.

"'The northernmost point where the wall curves slightly,'" she read aloud, scanning the harbour perimeter.

Maria pointed silently to where the straight wall gently bent outward, providing a wider viewing platform. They walked to it, their footsteps loud in the winter quiet.

Emma placed her hands on the cold stone, gazing out toward where the protected harbour opened to the Atlantic. "This is where she stood," she said softly. "Where she learned about endings and beginnings."

Rosie opened her handbag, touching the silver container

within, then closed it again. "Not yet," she whispered. "Dawn, like she asked."

Maria pulled a slim notebook from her coat pocket, flipping to a page of handwritten notes. "Low tide begins at 6:17 AM," she said. "The fishing boats leave around 5:30, according to Mrs. Trewin."

They stood in silence, three figures against the darkening sky, feeling the presence of a fourth among them.

"I brought something," Emma said suddenly, reaching into her pocket. She produced a small flask and three collapsible cups. "For tomorrow. Lisa's favourite."

"Single malt," Rosie said with a knowing smile. "Eighteen years, neat."

"She always said life was too short for bad whisky," Maria added, accepting a cup.

"To tomorrow," Emma said, raising her cup toward the horizon where sea met sky in deepening twilight. "One last sunrise with our Lisa."

That evening, they went to The Fisherman's Arms, a pub nestled into the harbour wall. The low-ceilinged room was filled with locals, the air warm with conversation and the scent of hearty food. They chose a corner table, feeling both out of place and strangely at home.

"She would have loved this," Rosie said, raising her glass. "The authenticity of it."

"She would have corrected the grammar on the menu," Emma countered, which drew a laugh from all three of them.

As their food arrived, Emma noticed a man at the bar watching them with unconcealed curiosity. Tall, with salt-and-pepper hair and the weathered complexion of someone who worked outdoors, he had the kind of rugged features that prompted Emma to straighten her posture subtly.

"Don't even think about it," Maria murmured, following her gaze. "Lisa specifically warned you about local fishermen."

"I'm just being friendly," Emma protested, offering the stranger a smile. "We're visitors in search of local knowledge, after all."

To their surprise, the man picked up his drink and approached their table. "Forgive me for intruding," he said, his accent a melodic Cornish lilt, "but I couldn't help noticing you're not from around here."

"What gave us away?" Emma asked with a playful tilt of her head. "Our fashionable London attire or our bewildered tourist expressions?"

He laughed—a warm, generous sound. "Neither. It's just that we don't get many visitors this time of year. Most come in summer when the weather's kinder." He gestured to the empty chair at their table. "May I?"

Introductions were made—his name was Daniel—and conversation flowed easily. He was indeed a fisherman, though he also taught at the local school part-time. "Marine biology," he explained. "Trying to get the next generation to care about the ocean."

As they chatted, Rosie carefully steered the conversation toward their purpose in Port Isaac.

"We're here because of an old friend," she explained. "She passed away recently, and this place meant a great deal to her. She spent a summer here in her youth."

"Many do," Daniel nodded. "Summer romances under Cornish skies—it's a tradition around here."

"Her name was Lisa," Maria said, watching Daniel's face carefully. "Lisa Mack, though she might have used a different name back then."

The reaction was subtle—a slight narrowing of his eyes, a pause before he took another sip of his drink. "When would this have been?"

"Early 1960s," Rosie supplied. "She mentioned someone named James Porter. He made quite an impression on her."

Daniel set his glass down with deliberate care. "James Porter," he repeated, his voice suddenly tight with emotion. "That was my father."

The three women exchanged stunned glances.

"Your father?" Emma echoed.

Daniel nodded, studying them with new intensity. "Did you say her name was Lisa? Not Elizabeth?"

Maria leaned forward. "She sometimes used Elizabeth. How did you know that?"

A slow smile spread across Daniel's face, transforming him instantly. "All my life, I heard stories about the summer girl from London—Elizabeth with the dark eyes and sharp mind. Dad mentioned her often, especially after Mum died."

"They were together that summer?" Rosie asked.

"More than that," Daniel said. "According to family legend, they were madly in love. Dad wanted to marry her, but she had dreams beyond our little fishing village—university, a career. They parted ways at summer's end." He paused, taking in their rapt expressions. "Dad passed away ten years ago, but he never forgot her. Even named his boat after her—'Elizabeth's Dream.'"

Emma reached into her bag and retrieved Lisa's letter and photograph, carefully preserved in a plastic sleeve. "This is her, from that summer. And this is what she wrote about your father."

Daniel studied the photograph with wonder. "I've seen this before," he said quietly. "Or one just like it. Dad kept a photo of her in his wallet his entire life."

He read the letter, his eyes growing damp. "James Porter was his name—tall, broad-shouldered, with eyes the colour of the Atlantic after a storm..." He looked up, blinking rapidly. "That's exactly how my mother used to describe him."

"Your mother?" Maria asked gently.

"They married a few years after Elizabeth—Lisa—left. Had a good life together. But Dad always said there were two great loves in his life. Mum understood. She used to say some people leave footprints on your heart that never fade."

Daniel hesitated, then seemed to make a decision. "There's something I think you should see. Something that might explain why this place meant so much to your friend."

Outside, the night air was crisp with sea salt. Daniel led them along the harbour and up a winding path that climbed the cliff face. The moon was rising, casting silver light across the restless sea below. At the top, a small stone bench overlooked the cove, sheltered by a ancient, twisted tree.

"Dad built this bench the year after she left," Daniel explained. "Said it was where they used to meet. Every year on the anniversary of their parting, he'd come up here at sunrise with a pot of tea and two cups." His voice softened. "I never understood why two cups, until now."

Rosie ran her hand over the weathered stone. "Lisa's letter mentioned she returned here every year on that anniversary. I wonder if they ever..."

"Missed each other by hours, probably," Daniel said with a sad smile. "Dad always came at sunrise. If she came later..."

"She wrote about watching the fishermen heading out," Maria recalled. "That would have been after dawn."

"All those years," Emma murmured. "Both of them returning to the same spot, never knowing."

Daniel nodded toward the tree that sheltered the bench. Its trunk was broad, its bark scarred with decades of carved initials and messages. He pointed to a particular carving, the letters still distinct despite the years: "J + E" inside a heart, and beneath it, the words "Two paths, one heart."

"Dad carved that the summer they were together," Daniel explained. "But this—" he indicated a smaller carving just below it, the letters JDP in a careful hand "—this is what I wanted to show you."

The women leaned closer, puzzled.

"James David Porter," Daniel said. "My father's initials. But look at the style—that's not his handwriting. And it wasn't carved until years later."

Maria traced the letters gently. "You think Lisa did this?"

Daniel nodded. "And there's more. After dad died, I found a notebook among his things. It's a journal he kept that summer with Elizabeth. They wrote to each other in it—little notes, quotes, sketches. Shall I go and get it?"

"That would be great. Would you mind? Do you live far from here?"

"No, give me 10 minutes."

DANIEL OPENED the notebook to a marked page. "This entry is from the day before she left."

In faded ink, in handwriting they immediately recognised as a younger version of Lisa's elegant script:

James, my heart remains here even as the rest of me must go. Remember our promise—I will make something of this fire inside me, and one day, when I've proven myself, I'll return. Whatever paths we walk, know that you taught me the most important lesson—that passion without courage is just wishful thinking. All my love, until we meet again. E.

Beneath it, in a bolder, more urgent hand:

Elizabeth, I will be here, waiting. Whether it's a year or a lifetime. Whatever life brings, know that you've given me the courage to want more than I was born to. I will make you proud. Forever yours, James

Daniel turned the page. A pressed flower—long dried but still recognisable as a sea lavender—was carefully preserved between the pages.

"These were growing all around the bench that summer, according to Dad," Daniel explained. "But there's something else you should see."

He flipped through the journal to the very back. Tucked

inside the cover was a small, brittle envelope, yellowed with age. "I found this after he died, but I never opened it. It's addressed to him, but the handwriting..."

Emma gasped softly. "That's Lisa's handwriting."

Daniel handed her the envelope. "I think perhaps it belongs to you now."

With trembling fingers, Emma carefully opened the sealed envelope. Inside was a single sheet of paper, dated twenty years after that summer, and a small photograph.

The photo showed a much younger Lisa, holding a book—her first published work, judging by her proud expression. Written on the back in Lisa's hand: *James, I kept my promise. Did you keep yours? Still thinking of you, E.*

The note was brief but heartfelt:

My dear James,

I came to Port Isaac today, as I do every year. I saw you on your boat with your son—he has your eyes. I almost approached, but seeing the life you've built, the happiness you've found, I realised some chapters are meant to stay closed, however beautiful they might have been.

I wanted you to know that those weeks we shared changed everything for me. You taught me to believe in myself when no one else did. The family I came from saw only my failings; you saw my potential. When I doubt myself, which is more often than I'd care to admit, I think of you saying, "The ocean doesn't care where you came from—only if you're brave enough to face its storms."

I've faced many storms since we parted, but I've never forgotten how to be brave. That was your gift to me.

With eternal gratitude, Your Elizabeth

"He never opened it," Rosie whispered, wiping away tears.

"He was married, to mum, perhaps he was too scared to start communicating with her. Scared of the feelings it would bring up." Daniel said softly.

They sat in silence for a moment, absorbing the revelation of this hidden chapter in Lisa's life.

"I think I understand now," Maria said finally. "This isn't just where she had her heart broken. This is where she found her courage."

"Where she became the Lisa we knew," Emma added.

Daniel stood, gazing out over the moonlit harbour. "I'd be honoured to take you to the exact spot on the harbour wall tomorrow at sunrise, if that's when you're planning to..." he hesitated, searching for the right words.

"Say our final goodbye," Rosie supplied gently.

"Yes," Daniel nodded. "And perhaps—if you think she would have wanted it—we could place a small portion near this bench as well. So they could be together, in a way they never managed in life."

As they made their way back down to the village, the stars brilliant above them and the sound of the waves a constant whisper, Emma broke the companionable silence.

"I bet she knew," she said suddenly. "I bet Lisa knew we'd meet Daniel. That's why she sent us here—not just to understand where she began, but to complete the circle."

Rosie smiled through her tears. "One last surprise from our Lisa."

"One last adventure," Maria corrected softly. "And we've only just begun."

"Did he ever regret letting her go?" Rosie asked gently.

The man shrugged. "Dad wasn't one for regrets. But he kept a photograph, tucked in his wallet. Pretty girl with dark hair and a smile that lit up her whole face. That would've been your friend, I reckon."

That night, they gathered in Rosie's room, sharing a bottle of wine and talking about Lisa—not the Lisa they'd known in her final months, weakened by illness, but the vibrant, fearless woman who had shaped their lives in so many ways.

"I can just picture her here," Emma said, gesturing toward the harbour visible through the window. "Nineteen years old, full of ambition, probably terrifying the locals with her London ways."

"And that poor fisherman's son," Rosie added with a smile. "Completely smitten and completely out of his depth."

"But she came back," Maria said thoughtfully. "Year after year. That's the part I keep coming back to. Lisa, who was always moving forward, always onto the next thing, deliberately maintained this one connection to her past."

"Because it mattered," Emma said simply. "It shaped her. And Lisa never forgot anything that shaped her, for better or worse."

They rose before dawn, dressing warmly against the January chill. The village was silent as they made their way down to the harbour, their footsteps echoing on the cobblestones. The sky was just beginning to lighten in the east, a pale gold band above the dark horizon.

At the curved section of the harbour wall, they stood together, watching as the first fishing boats prepared to depart for the day's catch. The air was sharp with salt and seaweed, the gulls already wheeling overhead in anticipation.

Rosie opened her bag and removed the silver container. "Should we say something?" she asked, suddenly uncertain.

"Lisa would hate speeches," Emma said firmly. "But she'd approve of a toast."

She produced a silver flask from her coat pocket and passed it around. The whisky burned pleasantly as each woman took a sip, warming them against the morning chill.

As the sun breached the horizon, casting long golden fingers across the water, Rosie opened the container. With a gentle movement, she scattered a portion of Lisa's ashes over the wall, watching as the fine grey powder was caught by the breeze and carried out toward the sea.

"To Lisa," she said softly. "Who never stopped learning from love, both given and received."

"To Lisa," Emma echoed. "Who made fearlessness look easy, even when it wasn't."

"To Lisa," Maria completed the circle. "Who returned to her beginnings even as she kept moving forward."

They stood in silence as the last of the ashes disappeared, feeling both the weight of loss and the strange lightness that came with fulfilling Lisa's wishes. The tide was turning, the water rising to meet the dawn, and somewhere out beyond the harbour mouth, Lisa's physical remains were becoming one with the sea she had loved in her youth.

Later, they found Mrs. Baxter's Tea Room—still in business after all these years, though now run by Mrs. Baxter's granddaughter. The back table with the harbour view was available, and they ordered cream teas as instructed.

"To James Porter," Emma said, raising her teacup in a gesture that somehow managed to be both ironic and sincere. "Who taught our Lisa about heartbreak, and in doing so, helped create the woman we loved."

"And to us," Rosie added. "For having the wisdom to listen to Lisa's instructions, even after she's gone."

"One down," Maria said, patting her bag where the remaining two envelopes waited. "Two to go."

As they drove away from Port Isaac that afternoon, the winter sun low in the sky behind them, each woman carried a new piece of Lisa with her. The first envelope had revealed not just a destination for her ashes, but a hidden chapter of her life that had helped shape all that followed.

GHOSTS AND EMPTY HANGERS

The steam from Rosie's forgotten cup of Earl Grey curled upward, dissipating in the morning light that filtered through Lisa's curtains. The room remained exactly as Lisa had left it six months ago—a silk scarf draped carelessly over the bedpost, reading glasses perched atop a stack of well-thumbed paperbacks, the faint scent of her signature perfume still lingering in the air.

Rosie's fingers trailed across the spines of books on the shelf, pausing at a dog-eared copy of Austen's *Persuasion*. She pulled it out, a train ticket from their trip to Bath tucked between pages 67 and 68. The bookmark frozen in time, like everything else in this room.

"You've been standing there for twenty minutes."

Rosie started, nearly dropping the book. Emma leaned against the doorframe, arms folded across her chest, hair still damp from her morning shower.

"Have I?" Rosie slipped the book back into place. "I didn't realise..."

Emma crossed the room to stand beside her, surveying the untouched belongings. "We've all been doing it. Maria spent an hour in here yesterday, just sitting on the bed, staring out the window."

Outside, a magpie landed on the oak tree branch that scratched against the windowpane in high winds—a sound that used to drive Lisa to distraction. *"If no one else will trim that bloody branch,"* she would threaten, *"I'll do it myself with nail scissors."*

"I think it's time," Rosie said quietly, meeting Emma's gaze. Let's get Maria,

Neither needed to clarify what "it" was.

The floorboards in the hallway creaked, announcing Maria's approach before she appeared in the doorway, a stack of flattened cardboard boxes under one arm, a roll of packing tape in the other.

Emma plucked a box from Maria's arms, unfolding it with decisive snaps. "It's been months. Lisa would have had this sorted within a fortnight and told us to pull ourselves together."

"Complete with a lecture on the impracticality of sentimentality," Maria added, the ghost of a smile crossing her face.

"And the environmental impact of unused space," Rosie chimed in.

The three women stood in silence for a moment, the half-constructed box between them a catalyst for what lay ahead.

Emma squared her shoulders. "Right then. No more dithering. Let's make a start before we lose our nerve."

"WHAT ABOUT THIS?" Emma held up a cashmere jumper in a shade of emerald-green that had perfectly complemented Lisa's dark eyes.

"Charity shop pile," Maria said from her position by the wardrobe, where she was methodically removing hangers of blouses and dresses. "We agreed, remember? Keep one or two pieces each, donate the rest."

"But she loved this one." Emma rubbed the soft fabric between her fingers. "She wore it last Christmas when—"

"When she told Mrs Henderson her Christmas pudding had the structural integrity of a nuclear bunker but none of the taste?" Rosie supplied from her spot on the floor, sorting through a collection of shoes.

Emma snorted. "To be fair, you could have built foundations with that pudding."

"Precisely why we're keeping those memories, not the jumper," Maria said gently, holding out a cardboard box labelled 'Charity' in her neat handwriting.

Emma hesitated, then dropped the jumper into the box. "You're right. Someone else will love it as much as she did." She reached back into the wardrobe. "Oh! What about this atrocity?" She pulled out a violently patterned silk blouse with enormous shoulder pads.

"Good Lord," Rosie laughed. "I'd forgotten about that monstrosity."

"Milan, 1987," Maria recalled. "She insisted it was haute couture."

"It was haute something," Emma muttered, dangling it at arm's length. "Definitely charity shop. Let some drama student use it for an '80s revival."

As the morning wore on, the room transformed. Bags for the charity shop multiplied in the hallway. Treasured mementos were carefully wrapped and boxed for each of them—the first edition of *Pride and Prejudice* for Rosie, the vintage champagne collection for Emma, the Chanel suit for Maria. Books were sorted, jewellery divided according to Lisa's meticulous instructions.

"Look at this," Rosie called from the back of the wardrobe, pulling out a shoebox. Inside lay dozens of handwritten notes, birthday cards, and thank-you letters they had given Lisa over the years. "She kept all of these."

"Of course she did," Emma said softly. "Beneath all that prickly exterior, she was a sentimental old fool."

Maria picked up a Christmas card she'd given Lisa three years earlier, reading her own handwriting: *To the sister I never had but somehow found anyway. All my love, M.*

She cleared her throat, carefully returning the card to the box. "We should keep these. All of them."

By mid-afternoon, they paused for lunch, eating sandwiches perched on Lisa's now-bare mattress, surveying their progress.

"It feels..."

"Empty," Rosie finished for Emma.

"But not wrong," Maria added. "Just... different."

Emma brushed crumbs from her lap, then stood abruptly. "I've been thinking. About what comes next. For this room, I mean."

"We don't have to decide today," Rosie began.

"No, but we should start thinking about it." Emma paced the length of the room. "It doesn't make sense to leave it empty. Not when—" She stopped, seeming to choose her words carefully. "Not when there are others who might need it."

Maria looked up sharply. "What are you suggesting?"

"Julie," Emma said simply.

"The one whose husband—"

"Left her for his twenty-five-year-old fitness instructor? Yes, that Julie." Emma turned to face them. "She mentioned at the funeral that she would be looking for somewhere to live."

Maria set her half-eaten sandwich aside. "You think we should offer her Lisa's room?"

"Not right away," Emma clarified. "But eventually, yes. When we're ready."

Silence fell as they considered this suggestion, the echo of Lisa's absence suddenly acute once more.

"She'd approve, you know," Rosie said finally. "Lisa, I mean. She always said this house was too big for just the three of us."

"And Julie makes those incredible chocolate brownies," Emma added. "With the sea salt on top."

"That's your primary criteria for a potential housemate? Baking skills?" Maria asked, but the corner of her mouth twitched upward.

"Don't pretend you're not considering it too," Emma retorted.

Maria glanced around the half-emptied room. "We'd need to redecorate. New paint at the very least. Those curtains would have to go."

"We could do it together," Rosie suggested. "Make it... not Lisa's room anymore, but something new."

"A new beginning," Emma agreed. "For all of us."

THREE WEEKS LATER, the transformation was complete. Gone were the deep burgundy walls Lisa had favoured, replaced by a soft sage green. New curtains hung at the windows, cream-coloured with a subtle pattern. The distressed French furniture had been replaced with heavier pieces from the loft.

The three women stood in the doorway, admiring their handiwork.

"It looks..." Maria searched for the right word.

"Peaceful," Rosie supplied.

"Welcoming," Emma added.

They had kept one reminder of Lisa—a small watercolour of Port Isaac harbour that now hung beside the window, its blues and greys complementing the room's new palette.

"Do you think she'd like it?" Rosie asked.

Emma snorted. "She'd say the curtains were impractical and that we've been watching too much daytime telly."

"But she'd understand," Maria said quietly. "Why we needed to do this."

They lingered a moment longer, then by unspoken agreement, closed the door and made their way downstairs.

In the kitchen, Emma pulled four wine glasses from the cupboard and a bottle of Lisa's favourite red—one of several they'd set aside from her extensive collection.

"I'll just pour Lisa a small glass," she said, before filling theirs.

"I invited Julie for lunch next Sunday," she announced. "Just to catch up. Nothing official."

Maria raised an eyebrow but said nothing, accepting her glass.

"What?" Emma challenged. "I'm not saying we offer her the room on the spot. Just... put out feelers."

"'Put out feelers'?" Rosie echoed. "You make it sound like we're recruiting for MI5."

"Finding the right housemate is a delicate operation," Emma insisted. "Especially for... for what we have here."

What they had built together. What they had lost. What they were trying, in their own way, to preserve while also moving forward.

Rosie raised her glass. "To new beginnings, then. And to Lisa, who would have told us to get on with it months ago."

"To Lisa," the others echoed, glasses clinking gently.

Outside, the afternoon sun caught the last of the autumn leaves on the oak tree, setting them ablaze with gold. The branch that had annoyed Lisa so much tapped gently against the window of what had been her room, now transformed, waiting for new stories to unfold within its walls.

Inside, three women who had faced the worst kind of loss together sipped wine and began, tentatively, to plan for the future—just as their friend would have wanted them to.

SECRETS IN LAKE COMO

With their journey to Cornwall complete and their first mission fulfilled, the three women gathered in the living room to open the second envelope. The winter afternoon was fading into dusk, the early February darkness gathering outside the windows. Inside, the fire crackled in the grate, casting a warm glow over them as they settled onto the sofa.

"Shall I?" Maria asked, lifting the sealed envelope from the coffee table.

Rosie nodded. "Go ahead."

With careful fingers, Maria broke the wax seal and extracted the contents. This photograph was larger than the first, a glossy colour print that captured Lisa in her prime. She stood on a stone balcony, the azure waters of what could only be an Italian lake shimmering behind her. Lisa wore a vintage gown that seemed to float around her—layers of ethereal midnight-blue silk that caught the golden hour light. Her dark hair was swept up elegantly, and she held a champagne flute aloft, her smile radiant and knowing, as if sharing a private joke with the photographer.

"That's Valentino," Rosie said decisively, peering at the dress through her reading glasses. "Late seventies, if I'm not mistaken. Worth a small fortune, especially now."

"How on earth did she afford something like that?" Emma wondered, reaching for the photograph.

"The more relevant question," Maria said, "is where was this taken? The landscape is stunning."

The background revealed glimpses of cypress trees, distant mountains, and that remarkable blue water. No identifying landmarks were visible, just the ornate stone balustrade of the balcony and a partial view of what appeared to be a grand villa.

Maria flipped the photo over. In Lisa's elegant script was written: *Where Alessandra's truth became art. Find the balcony where scandals were born and champagne flowed like water.*

"Alessandra?" Emma frowned. "Another pseudonym?"

"Or a person," Rosie suggested. "Lisa wrote several autobiographies for fashion figures. Was one of them called Alessandra?"

Maria snapped her fingers. "Alessandra Visconti! The muse of Marco Roselli. Lisa wrote that explosive biography about ten years ago—*The Designer's Shadow*. It caused quite a stir in the fashion world."

"I remember now," Emma said. "Marco Roselli was that Italian designer who was enormously influential in the seventies and eighties. Lisa's book revealed he had stolen many of his breakthrough designs from his collaborators."

"And Alessandra was one of them," Rosie added, memories clicking into place. "The book transformed how fashion history viewed Roselli's legacy."

Emma studied the photograph again. "So this must be in Italy. That water—it has to be one of the lakes. Como, perhaps?"

"Let me see," Maria said, taking the photograph back. She examined the balustrade with careful eyes. "These stone carvings are distinctive. Cherubs and grapevines... very characteristic of the villas around Lake Como."

"Wow, how did you know that?"

"It says here," said Maria, with a smile, lifting her finger to reveal a small note in the bottom right hand corner on the back of the picture.

For the next three weeks, the women immersed themselves in research. Emma's laptop became a permanent fixture on the coffee table, and Maria created an elaborate timeline on the kitchen wall charting Marco Roselli's career and the publication of Lisa's biography.

They learned that *The Designer's Shadow* had been published in 2010, five years after Marco Roselli's death, causing a seismic shift in the fashion world's understanding of his work. Before the book, Alessandra Visconti had been considered merely his muse and occasional model; after, she was recognised as the uncredited genius behind many of his most celebrated designs.

"The flights to Milan are booked," Emma announced one evening, closing her laptop with a flourish. "We leave next Thursday."

"So soon?" Rosie looked up from the fashion history book she'd been skimming.

"April is perfect for Lake Como," Maria replied, consulting her weather charts. "Not too hot, not too cold, and fewer tourists than summer."

Emma raised her glass. "To our second adventure with Lisa. May it be as revealing as the first."

"And hopefully much sunnier," Rosie added with a smile.

THE TRANSITION from English winter to Italian spring couldn't have been more dramatic. As their plane descended toward Milan, the landscape below had changed from muted greys to vibrant greens, the Alps still snow-capped in the distance.

The Italian spring had arrived and Lake Como looked beautiful. Wildflowers dotted the hillsides, and the lake itself was a mirror reflecting the surrounding mountains and the cloudless blue sky above. The air smelled of wisteria and jasmine, carried on the gentle breeze.

"According to my research," Maria said as they sipped espresso at a lakeside café, "the villa is on the western shore, about twenty minutes north by boat."

"And how exactly do we get access to a private villa owned by a woman who famously avoids visitors?" Emma asked.

"I've been giving that some thought," Rosie replied. "In my experience, even the most reclusive people respond to a direct, respectful approach. We simply tell her the truth."

"That we're scattering the ashes of a friend who once visited her father's villa?" Maria questioned. "Why would she care?"

"Because Lisa's book changed her father's legacy forever," Emma said quietly. "For better or worse, Sophia Roselli lives in the shadow of both her father and Lisa's revelations about him. She might be curious enough to grant us a brief visit."

They arranged for a water taxi to take them as close to the villa as possible. As they cut across the lake, the spray occasionally dampening their faces, the grandeur of the landscape was breathtaking. Elegant villas dotted the shoreline, their gardens cascading down to the water.

The driver pointed out Villa Celestina as they approached—a pale yellow structure with white columns, partially hidden behind tall cypress trees and surrounded by terraced gardens. It was smaller than they had imagined, but undeniably exquisite, with the particular grace of a building designed to be admired from the water.

"The signoria does not receive visitors," the driver informed them as he dropped them at the nearest public dock.

"Many have tried to see the villa since the book was published."

The women thanked him and made their way up a narrow lane that led toward the villa's main entrance. Climbing stone steps bordered by flowering shrubs, they reached a high wall with a wrought-iron gate. A security camera pivoted toward them as they approached.

Rosie pressed the intercom button beside the gate. After a long moment, a woman's voice answered in Italian.

"Mi dispiace, la villa non è aperta al pubblico."

"We're friends of Lisa Mack," Rosie replied. "We've come from England regarding a personal matter."

Silence followed, so prolonged they began to think they'd been dismissed. Then the voice returned, now in perfect English.

"Lisa Mack is dead. It was in the papers."

"Yes," Maria said, stepping closer to the intercom. "She left instructions for us to visit places that were significant to her. This villa is one of them."

Another long pause.

"Wait there."

Ten minutes passed before the gates finally opened. A silver-haired woman in her sixties, impeccably dressed in linen trousers and a silk blouse, stood in the driveway. Her resemblance to Marco Roselli was subtle but unmistakable—the same high cheekbones and penetrating gaze.

"I am Sophia Roselli," she said, her voice cool and measured. "You said you were friends of Lisa Mack?"

"Yes," Rosie confirmed. "I'm Rosie, and these are Emma and Maria."

Sophia studied them with unreadable eyes. "What is this about her ashes?"

Maria explained Lisa's final request—the three photographs, the mission to scatter her ashes in places that had meaning to her. As she spoke, Sophia's expression remained guarded, but something shifted in her eyes.

"Show me this photograph," she said finally.

Emma handed it over. Sophia examined it carefully, her finger tracing the outline of the balustrade.

"The Celestina Terrace," she said quietly. "It hasn't been used for events in many years." She looked up at them. "Why was this villa important to her?"

The women exchanged glances.

"We believe it's connected to her biography of your father," Rosie said carefully. "And perhaps to Alessandra Visconti."

A flicker of emotion crossed Sophia's face. "I see. And you wish to scatter her ashes here?"

"If possible," Emma said. "On the balcony in the photograph."

Sophia handed the photograph back. "That section of the villa is closed. The terrace is not structurally sound."

"Is there no way we could work out a way to do this? Maybe just one of us should go up there?"

"No," she said, beginning to walk away.

"We have come a long way. We are trying to honour the last wishes of a dear friend."

Sophia hesitated, then added, " Follow me."

She led them through a side garden, where the scent of roses hung heavy in the air. The villa itself was even more beautiful up close, its walls weathered to a soft patina, vines climbing around the windows. Inside, they glimpsed high ceilings, original frescoes, and furnishings that spoke of old wealth and refined taste.

They followed a corridor lined with black-and-white photographs—fashion shoots from different eras, all featuring Marco Roselli's designs. At the end of the hall, Sophia unlocked a set of French doors.

"The terrace has been closed for five years," she explained, "ever since part of the balustrade collapsed during a storm. Please be careful."

They stepped onto the terrace and immediately recognised it from the photograph. The view was identical—the same sweep of lake, the distant mountains, the particular angle of light on the water. The stone balustrade was indeed damaged in places, with temporary barriers erected along one section.

"This is definitely it," Maria breathed, comparing the photograph to the real view.

Sophia watched them with guarded curiosity. "You don't know why she chose this place, do you?"

Rosie shook her head. "We're discovering new aspects of Lisa's life with each location. She was... more complex than we realised."

A hint of a smile touched Sophia's lips. "Lisa Mack was many things. Predictable was not one of them." She gestured to a door on the far side of the terrace. "Come. There is someone you should meet."

They followed her through the door and into a bright sitting room overlooking another section of the garden. An elderly woman sat in a wheelchair by the window, her white hair elegantly styled, her hands adorned with beautiful rings. Though age had softened her features, there was no mistaking the striking bone structure and commanding presence of Alessandra Visconti.

"We have visitors, Alessandra," Sophia said, her voice gentler than before. "Friends of Lisa Mack."

Alessandra's eyes—still remarkably vibrant and intelligent at eighty-three—widened with surprise. "Lisa?" she repeated, her accent thick but her English clear. "You knew my Lisa?"

The three women approached, introducing themselves. As Maria explained their mission again, Alessandra's expression shifted from surprise to deep emotion.

"Sit, please," she said, gesturing to the chairs arranged nearby. "Sophia, would you bring Lisa's letters?"

Sophia nodded and left the room.

"You live here?" Maria asked, surprised.

Alessandra smiled. "For ten years now. Since my apartment in Milan became too difficult with the stairs. Sophia invited me to stay."

"That's very kind," Emma said, glancing at the doorway through which Sophia had disappeared.

"Not kind. Family," Alessandra corrected. "Sophia is my daughter."

The revelation hung in the air as the women processed its implications. Before they could respond, Sophia returned carrying a wooden box.

"My mother and Marco Roselli were together for many years," she explained, placing the box beside Alessandra. "Though never publicly acknowledged."

"And my designs were his greatest successes," Alessandra added without bitterness. "This was the way of the fashion world then. Men received the credit; women did the work."

"Which is what Lisa revealed in her biography," Rosie said.

Alessandra nodded. "Lisa came here first in 1992, for a retrospective of Marco's work. She was writing for fashion magazines then, not yet famous for her biographies." She opened the box, revealing dozens of letters tied with faded ribbon. "She returned many times over the years. We became... very close."

The meaning behind her words was unmistakable.

"You and Lisa were lovers," Emma said gently.

"For nearly fifteen years," Alessandra confirmed. "Always in secret. She had her life in London; I had my obligations here. But twice a year, we would meet at this villa." She lifted out a bundle of letters. "She was brilliant, passionate, uncompromising—everything I admired."

"The biography," Maria prompted. "Was it your idea?"

"It was Lisa's gift to me," Alessandra said. "After Marco died in 2005, there was no longer a need for secrecy about my work. The designs were mine; the world deserved to know." She caressed the letters with tender fingers. "She spent months here, interviewing me, examining original sketches, building the case meticulously. When *The Designer's Shadow* was published in 2010, the fashion establishment was furious, but the truth prevailed."

"The dress," Emma said suddenly, reaching for the photograph they'd brought with them. "It looks so much like a Valentino from that period."

Alessandra smiled, a hint of pride in her eyes. "Many people made that mistake. Marco asked me to design something in Valentino's style for a private collection. It was never credited to me, of course, but it was mine entirely." She touched the image gently. "Lisa loved the story behind it—how something could appear to be one thing while actually being another. She borrowed it whenever she visited."

"So Rosie was right about it being a Valentino design," Maria observed, "but not an official one."

"The highest form of flattery in fashion is successful imitation," Alessandra replied with a wink. "Though I'd never admit that publicly."

Sophia returned with a tray of prosecco and delicate glasses. "It changed my understanding of my father," she said, pouring the sparkling wine.

They raised their glasses in a toast to Lisa, the bubbles catching the light just as they had in the photograph taken decades earlier on the terrace.

"Would you like to see the gown?" Alessandra asked suddenly. "The one from the photograph? Lisa left it here, said it belonged with its designer."

Later, as the golden hour approached—the same magical

light captured in the photograph—they gathered on the terrace. Emma opened the crystal container holding a portion of Lisa's ashes. With Alessandra and Sophia looking on, the three women scattered them over the damaged balustrade, watching as the breeze carried the fine ash out over the shimmering waters of Lake Como.

"To Lisa," Rosie said, raising her glass. "Who revealed truth through her words."

"Who loved passionately," added Emma.

"Who connected worlds," Maria finished.

As the sun began to set, casting the lake in shades of amber and rose, Alessandra handed Rosie a small package wrapped in tissue paper.

"Letters," she explained. "Copies of some of ours. So you can know the Lisa I knew—the romantic, the dreamer, the woman who loved beautiful things and beautiful truths in equal measure."

Their journey back to England was quiet, each woman absorbed in her thoughts, processing this new dimension of their friend. The Lisa who had lived a passionate secret romance for fifteen years with an Italian designer. The Lisa who had used her formidable talents as a biographer not just to advance her career, but to secure a rightful place in history for a woman whose genius had been overshadowed.

"I'm beginning to think," Rosie said thoughtfully, "that Lisa designed these journeys for us as carefully as Alessandra designed that gown. Each one revealing a different thread of who she was."

"And we're only just learning how to see the complete pattern," Emma added.

In their shared house in Esher, with two photographs now fulfilled and one remaining, they felt closer to Lisa than they had when she was alive—as if in death, she was finally allowing them to know her fully, in all her brilliant, complex entirety.

BROKEN BEAUTIFUL

A soft rain pattered against the windows of the Esher house, creating rivulets that distorted the garden view outside. The women had gathered for what had become something of a ritual—the opening of another envelope, the final stage of their posthumous journey with their friend.

With two photographs now fulfilled—Cornwall's fishing village and Lake Como's secret romance—only one adventure remained. Emma held the last sealed envelope in her hands, turning it over as if its weight contained more than just paper and possibility.

"Hard to believe this is the last one," she said, voice unusually subdued.

Maria and Rosie settled into the leather armchairs that flanked the fireplace, teacups balanced on the arms. The rain intensified, drumming against the glass like impatient fingers.

"Well, go on then," Rosie urged gently. "We've crossed England and Italy already. Where is she sending us for the grand finale?"

Emma broke the seal and withdrew the final photograph. The image was simpler than the others—a worn, slightly faded colour print of Lisa sitting on a weathered bench along Brighton's famous promenade. She wore a cream linen dress and a wide-brimmed straw hat, her face caught in profile as she gazed out to sea. Nothing remarkable, except for the expression on Lisa's face—a soft, contented smile they rarely saw in her everyday life or even at the glamorous Italian villa.

"There's something different about her here," Emma observed, passing the photograph to Maria. "She looks... at peace with herself."

Rosie took the photograph, turning it over. In Lisa's elegant handwriting was written: *Where Elizabeth found her true voice. Look to the pier where broken things become beautiful.*

Maria took back the photo, studying it with careful eyes. "The bench she's sitting on—you can just make out part of a plaque. It looks like it says 'Second Chance.'"

Rosie retrieved a magnifying glass from Lisa's desk drawer and handed it to Maria, who examined the photograph more closely.

"You're right," she said finally. "'Second Chance Memorial Bench.' And there's something else—look at what she's holding in her lap. It's not a book. It's a sketchpad."

"Lisa couldn't draw to save her life," Emma said, frowning. "She once tried to sketch my profile and it looked like a potato with hair. Remember that monstrosity she drew at our art night. Poor John Collins had all sorts of physical ailments in that picture."

Maria tapped her fingers on the desk, thinking. "The writing says 'where Elizabeth found her true voice.' Lisa was a writer—her voice was her words. Perhaps there's a different side to her? A side we never knew?"

Rosie's eyes widened. "You think she had some secret artistic talent she never shared with us?"

"I don't know," Maria said. "But Brighton's famous for art

and creativity. Let's search through her things for any connection to Brighton beyond this photograph."

For hours, they searched through the boxes that were piled up in the spare room. They combed through Lisa's papers but nothing pointed to a secret artistic life until Emma held her hand aloft.

"Look at this," she said, holding up a small, well-worn business card. "Brighton Art Therapy Collective. And there's a name written on the back—Dr. Samira Patel."

As Emma said the name, Rosie snapped her fingers. "Patel! That's a name I've heard before." She disappeared into the spare room, returning moments later with a file. "Here—among the papers about the Harrington biography."

"The Harrington affair," Maria murmured. "I'd almost forgotten about that."

Emma looked up. "That was what, 2008? 2009? Lisa rarely talked about it."

"With good reason," Rosie said, scanning the documents. "Sir William Harrington—former cabinet minister, respected statesman, and apparently, according to Lisa's biography, a man who made his fortune through insider trading and exploiting government connections."

"I remember now," Maria said. "He sued her for libel. It was all over the papers."

"The case dragged on for nearly two years," Rosie continued, reading. "Harrington had powerful friends. Publishers dropped her, commissions dried up. Even though she eventually won the case and was vindicated, the damage to her reputation was done."

"And Dr. Patel?" Emma asked, examining the business card.

"Here," Rosie tapped a letter. "Lisa's GP referred her to Dr. Patel for depression during the lawsuit. That must be the connection to Brighton."

The next morning found them driving to Brighton, the

seaside city resplendent under a surprisingly clear February sky. Gulls wheeled overhead as they parked near the famous pier, its Victorian ironwork silhouetted against the horizon. The scent of salt and vinegar from a nearby chip shop mingled with the briny sea air, and the distant calls of arcade games floated on the breeze.

"The address for the Art Therapy Collective is just off the Lanes," Maria said, consulting her phone. "About a ten-minute walk from here."

They followed the cobbled pathways of Brighton's famous Lanes, passing colourful boutiques and quirky cafés until they reached a converted Georgian townhouse with large windows and a discreet plaque reading "Brighton Art Therapy Collective."

Inside, the reception area displayed a stunning array of artwork—not the polished pieces one might find in a gallery, but raw, emotional works that spoke of pain, healing, and hope.

"Can I help you?" asked a young woman at the reception desk.

"We're looking for Dr. Samira Patel," Rosie explained. "It's about a former... client, perhaps? Lisa Mack?"

The receptionist's expression brightened with recognition. "Oh, wonderful. How is she?"

"I'm afraid she died."

The receptionist was visibly shaken. "I'm so sorry. What awful news. Let me see whether Dr. Patel is available."

Minutes later, they were ushered into a warm, sunlit studio where a striking woman in her fifties with silver-streaked black hair was arranging paintbrushes. The room smelled of linseed oil and turpentine, with splashes of colour adorning every surface.

"Lisa's friends," she said with a gentle smile. "Do come in. I was so sorry to read of Lisa's death. That horrible tumour. Terrible."

"So, you knew she was ill?" Maria asked.

"Yes," Dr. Patel nodded. "It's partly why she wanted to complete her project before..." She paused. "But I'm getting ahead of myself. You've come about Elizabeth, haven't you?"

"Elizabeth was Lisa?" Rosie asked.

Dr. Patel gestured for them to sit. "In a manner of speaking. Lisa came to us fifteen years ago, during a particularly difficult period in her life. She'd been diagnosed with depression following the Harrington lawsuit that nearly destroyed her career and reputation."

"We've just learned about that," Emma said quietly. "She never told us how deeply it affected her."

"Lisa was a master at concealing her wounds," Dr. Patel said. "She came here originally for conventional therapy, but I suggested she try our art therapy program as well. She insisted she had no artistic talent, but that's not what art therapy is about. It's about expression, not skill."

"And she took to it?" Maria asked, surprised.

"Not at first," Dr. Patel smiled. "She was resistant, analytical, wanted to intellectualize everything. But gradually, something began to change." She rose and walked to a cabinet, retrieving a portfolio. "She began working on a graphic memoir of sorts. Not for publication—for healing. She called it 'Elizabeth's Journey.'"

She opened the portfolio to reveal a series of amateur but powerfully evocative drawings. The early ones were dark, chaotic, filled with sharp angles and heavy shadows. As they progressed, light began to appear, first as tiny breaks in the darkness, then gradually expanding.

"Elizabeth was the name she gave to the part of herself she'd lost touch with," Dr. Patel explained. "The vulnerable, creative, non-analytical part that didn't care about status or professional reputation."

"She never mentioned any of this," Rosie said, tears welling in her eyes as she touched one of the drawings—a simple sketch of hands reaching toward light.

"She was intensely private about it. Said it was the one part of her life that wasn't tangled up in expectations—others' or her own." Dr. Patel turned more pages, revealing increasingly colourful and hopeful images. "She came to Brighton every month for years. Said the sea air helped her think differently."

Emma pointed to a drawing of a bench on the promenade— the same one from the photograph. "What's the significance of this bench?"

"The Second Chance bench? It was where she made a decision," Dr. Patel said. "After the Harrington verdict finally came through in her favour in 2010, Lisa had to decide whether to return to writing. She felt her reputation was irreparably damaged, that she'd never work again. On that bench, she decided to continue—but on her own terms."

"That timing aligns perfectly," Maria said thoughtfully. "Her biography of Marco Roselli and Alessandra Visconti was published later that same year. It was her comeback."

"And the pier?" Rosie asked, remembering the clue. "Something about broken things becoming beautiful?"

Dr. Patel smiled, leading them to the window that overlooked the seafront. In the distance, the skeletal remains of Brighton's West Pier were visible, standing in stark silhouette against the sky.

"Brighton's West Pier was damaged beyond repair in a fire years ago. Rather than demolish it completely, the city left its skeletal structure standing in the sea. At sunset, it creates one of the most photographed silhouettes in England—a broken thing that found new purpose as art."

"Like Lisa found a new purpose through her art therapy," Rosie said quietly.

"Exactly. But there's more to the story." Dr. Patel led them to another room, where a striking mosaic covered one wall—a sunset over the sea, with the skeletal pier in silhouette. "Two years ago, after her diagnosis, Lisa came to me with a proposal. She wanted to create something permanent, something that might help others."

"She made this?" Emma asked incredulously.

"Not alone. This was a group project involving over thirty people from our trauma survivor program. Lisa funded it anonymously and worked alongside people who had experienced everything from bereavement to abuse to illness. She called it 'Broken Beautiful.'"

Upon closer inspection, they could see that the mosaic was made from thousands of tiny fragments—broken china, sea glass, bits of mirror, each catching the light differently as they moved around the room.

"Every piece was contributed by someone in the program," Dr. Patel explained. "Items that represented their trauma, transformed into something beautiful. Lisa's pieces are here." She pointed to several fragments of what appeared to be expensive fountain pens. "From the pen she used to write the Harrington biography. And these—" she indicated some white and blue porcelain pieces, "from a teacup gifted to her by her birth mother."

Maria gasped softly. "She broke her mother's teacup?"

"To heal," Dr. Patel corrected gently. "To acknowledge that even precious things can be transformed when broken. That was the lesson Lisa said she most needed to learn—that broken doesn't mean ruined. Let me show you the note from her that went with it..."

Brighton was my sanctuary when I believed my career, my very identity, was destroyed. The Harrington scandal broke me in ways I couldn't admit. I came here intending to reinvent myself, to become someone new. Instead, I discovered parts of myself I'd long buried—the vulnerability I thought weakness, the playfulness I'd sacrificed for professionalism, the capacity to create without words.

Dr. Patel once asked me why I kept this part of my life secret from those closest to me. The truth was embarrassingly simple: I was afraid no one would accept this version of me. That everyone prefered the polished, articulate Lisa to the fumbling, expressive Elizabeth.

What I learned too late was that we all contain multitudes. That the cracks in our armour aren't flaws—they're where the light gets in. I wish I'd shared Elizabeth with the world sooner.

They spent the afternoon walking Brighton's promenade, following in Lisa's footsteps. They found the Second Chance bench and sat where she had sat, watching the waves crash against the shore. They explored the quirky shops of the Lanes, where Lisa had likely browsed after her therapy sessions. In a small café overlooking the sea, they shared memories of their friend, connecting the dots between the Cornwall Lisa, the Lake Como Lisa, and now the Brighton Lisa—three facets of a complex, remarkable woman.

"It's like pieces of a mosaic," Maria observed, stirring her tea. "Each location revealing another fragment of who she truly was."

"And we never saw the full picture while she was alive," Emma added.

"She compartmentalised her life so completely," Rosie said. "I wonder how exhausting that must have been for her."

The afternoon light began to soften as they made their way back to the Brighton Art Therapy Collective. Dr. Patel was waiting with three small velvet pouches.

"Fragments from the mosaic," she explained, handing one to each of them. "Send them off with her."

"Thank you," Rosie said, carefully tucking the pouch into her handbag. "Not just for this, but for being there for Lisa when she needed it most."

"She did the same for many others," Dr. Patel replied. "That was her gift—turning her own pain into purpose."

That evening, as the sun began its descent, they stood on

Brighton Pier. The crystal container holding a quarter of Lisa's ashes rested in Rosie's hands. The scent of candyfloss and salt water filled the air, while seagulls wheeled overhead against the deepening sky.

"It's like she planned everything," Emma said softly, turning the colourful fragment in her hand. "Even to the last detail. Cornwall, Lake Como, and now Brighton—three places, three Lisas."

"That was Lisa," Rosie replied. "Always in control."

"Except here," Maria said thoughtfully. "Here she learned to let go."

As the sun touched the horizon, bathing the skeletal remains of the West Pier in golden light, they scattered Lisa's ashes, watching as they drifted down to meet the sea. With them went the mosaic fragments, catching the light as they fell—broken pieces transformed one last time as they merged with the waves.

For a moment, none of them spoke, each lost in thought about the friend they'd known through her resilient beginning in Cornwall, her passionate romance in Italy, and now the vulnerable artist in Brighton—three facets of a woman more complex than they had ever realized while she lived.

"I wish we'd known this side of her," Rosie said finally. "I wish she'd felt she could share it."

"Perhaps that's the final lesson," Maria suggested. "To share all of ourselves with those we love, before it's too late."

"Or perhaps," Emma added, watching the last light glint off the broken pier, "it's that it's never too late to discover new parts of ourselves. Lisa did that right until the end."

They remained on the pier until twilight. When they finally turned to leave, each carried away something more valuable than memories—a reminder that healing often comes in unexpected forms, and that even the most familiar people can contain unknown depths.

As they drove back to Esher, Emma said suddenly, "You

know what we should do? Take one of those art therapy classes ourselves."

"Us? Making art?" Maria looked sceptical.

"Why not?" Emma grinned. "Lisa would love the irony of her perfectly composed friends making a glorious mess with paint."

"I think she'd love it, full stop," Rosie said. "She'd see it as us getting to know Elizabeth at last."

As Brighton faded in the rearview mirror, they fell into a comfortable silence. The journey with Lisa was complete. The only problem was that a quarter of the ashes remained.

SUNFLOWERS AND SECRETS

The warmth of the autumn sun lay soft across the rolling cemetery. It was the kind of day that it was impossible not to love. Everything about the world felt better when the weather was like this. The *feeling* of it was wonderful, the kind that soaked into your skin and whispered: *You're still here. Make it count.*

Rosie bent down at the grave and placed a bouquet of radiant sunflowers at the foot of the headstone. Their bright yellow faces turned unashamedly skyward.

"You always said they were like little suns," she murmured, her voice low and fond. "Lighting up any old dreary room. Just like you."

Maria gave a short, throaty chuckle. "She'd be rolling her eyes at us now. 'Three old hens clucking around my grave'—that's what she'd say."

Emma snorted, tugging her peacock-feather scarf into place. "Speak for yourself. I'm a flamingo, darling. Elegant, tall, and slightly ridiculous."

Their laughter danced through the cool air, startling a nearby blackbird from its perch. Even the cemetery, with its rows of greying stone and whispering trees, seemed to pause to listen.

Rosie rose slowly, brushing specks of earth from her knees, and glanced at her friends. "Well, shall we fill her in?"

They linked arms—habitual now, their small circle of strength—and stood shoulder to shoulder like sentinels in technicolour. Emma's coat was cherry red, Maria wore indigo with sunflower earrings, and Rosie had draped herself in a shawl Lisa had given her: crimson silk with gold thread, worn and beautiful.

Maria cleared her throat dramatically. "Lisa, you won't believe it but I've started dressing nicely every day – make up, jewellery everything. Like you always said – you never know what each day will bring. I'll be honest, the days haven't brought much so far, other than lotas of expensive cleanser and more ironing, but I'm keeping at it, and I think of you every time I get dressed."

Rosie's expression softened. "I've got five clients now. Gardening. Actual money. I always think of you when I'm elbow-deep in soil. You said I had green thumbs and a mushy heart, like some romantic Victorian botanist."

Emma hesitated, then smiled. "I'm painting again. Like you always said I should. Why didn't I listen to you? Not just once a week—every day. I even sold one last month, can you imagine? A lady from Truro cried when she saw it. Said it reminded her of a lost summer in St Ives. I felt... connected, somehow. To her. To you."

There was silence then, not awkward or empty, but full— rich with unspoken memories.

The headstone was simple, as Lisa had wanted. No dates, no grand epitaph. Just her name, and one of her own lines engraved in delicate script: *"Live like your heart's on fire."*

Maria reached out and traced the letters with a gloved finger. "A year ago, we didn't know each other properly. Not like we do now. We were housemates. But Lisa changed all that."

"She made us family," Emma said. "She pulled the truth out of us, piece by piece. Like it was a game."

"She pulled the truth out of herself, too," Rosie added. "Even if she waited until the very end."

They were quiet again. The breeze lifted a golden leaf and sent it tumbling across the grave like a dancer in a silk gown.

"She was outrageous," Maria said softly. "So full of contradictions. Glamorous and scruffy. Generous and ruthless. She'd lend you her lipstick and call you a twit in the same breath."

"She made life *big*," Emma said. "Even when she was shrinking away."

A robin landed near the headstone, cocking its head at them. Rosie watched it, chest tight.

"Do you remember the night we lit the fire pit and read her old columns aloud?" she asked. "We laughed so hard we woke the neighbours."

"She'd have approved," Maria said. "Ruffling feathers from beyond the grave."

"And that story about the German publisher?" Emma added, grinning now. "What was his name again—Fritz?"

"No – Hans, wasn't it?" Maria corrected with a sly smile. "Lisa's secret lover in Berlin. I still can't believe she kept that from us."

"Wrote him letters on real paper," Rosie added. "In German, no less."

Maria sighed. "I read them. Every word. They were... exquisite. She was in love. Not just with him—with the whole damn *idea* of him. Romance, mystery, Europe. It was the one part of her life she didn't share, until the very end."

They glanced at each other—three women with crow's feet and bright eyes, with second chances and unfinished stories.

They had arrived feeling broken in different ways. Now they stood whole, if slightly cracked. Beautiful in a different light.

Rosie stepped forward one last time. "We miss you," she whispered. "Every day. But we're living now, not just waiting. Just like you wanted."

As they turned to go, Emma looped her arms around the others, resting her cheek briefly on Maria's shoulder. "She'd say we're fabulous, wouldn't she?"

Maria smiled through tears. "She'd say we're still *hers*."

They walked slowly back to the car, the gravel crunching beneath their boots, each of them lost in thought. Behind them, the grave lay bright with sunflowers and stories.

That evening, back at the house, the golden hour streamed into the kitchen. Maria stirred something garlicky on the stove, Emma set the table with vintage napkins folded into elaborate fans, and Rosie uncorked a bottle of Lisa's favourite red.

"I spoke to Alessandra today," Rosie said, pouring with care. "She's coming to visit next month. She wants to see where Lisa lived. To feel close to her again."

Emma nodded. "I hope she tells us more. There's still so much of Lisa left to discover."

They raised their glasses.

"To Lisa," Rosie said. "To stories. To second acts."

"To love," Maria added.

"To flamingos and hens and peacocks," Emma said with a wink.

Their laughter filled the room—bold, irreverent, defiant.

Just as Lisa would have liked.

As they sat down to dinner, the golden evening light streamed through the windows, casting long shadows across the dining room. The house felt warm, alive, filled with the energy of three women who had faced loss together and emerged stronger for it.

"To Lisa," Rosie said, raising her glass. "Who continues to guide us, even now."

"To Lisa," the others echoed.

The evening passed in easy companionship, in shared stories and gentle laughter. Later, as Emma and Maria cleared the dishes, Rosie wandered into Lisa's study, drawn there by a feeling she couldn't quite name.

Then something caught Rosie's eye—a small, flat package on the desk that hadn't been there earlier. It was wrapped in cream-coloured paper and tied with a familiar red ribbon, the kind Lisa had always used for special gifts.

"Emma? Maria?" Rosie called. "Did either of you leave something on Lisa's desk?"

They both appeared in the doorway, looking puzzled.

"Not me," Emma said.

"Nor me," Maria added. "What is it?"

Rosie picked up the package carefully. "I'm not sure. It looks like one of Lisa's gifts, but..."

With fingers that trembled slightly, she untied the ribbon and removed the wrapping paper. Inside was a slender book bound in soft blue leather, its cover embossed with a simple gold design—a lighthouse beam stretching across dark waters.

"It's beautiful," Maria breathed, moving closer.

Rosie opened the cover. On the first page, in Lisa's distinctive handwriting, was an inscription:

For my Sensational Sixties Squad, My final gift, to be discovered when you've travelled all three paths. Three journeys completed, one yet to begin. Turn the page when you're ready for your next adventure. With all my love, Lisa

The three women stared at each other, a mixture of surprise, wonder, and the faintest touch of apprehension in their expressions.

"How on earth..." Emma began.

"She must have hidden it," Maria suggested. "Arranged for

someone to place it here after we completed the three photograph journeys."

"But who?" Rosie wondered.

Emma shook her head. "That's not the right question. The right question is: what's on the next page?"

They gathered closer as Rosie carefully turned the delicate page. What they saw made them all gasp in unison.

It was a photograph—not a faded vintage image like the others, but a relatively recent one. It showed a whitewashed village clinging to a hillside, the Mediterranean Sea sparkling in the background. And there, just visible in one corner, was Lisa standing beside a blue door with her arm around a dark-haired woman neither of them recognised.

On the facing page, more of Lisa's handwriting:

Deià, Majorca. Where my true story began. Where Elisabeta Montero became Lisa Mack after being given up for adoption by Sarah. The final piece awaits you there. Enjoy looking for the blue door, but also enjoy the sunshine and the dancing, dress up, flirt and get yourselves kissed on a holiday of a lifetime. And – also – throw the final quarter of me across that beautiful land. Make sure you go in June for the Sant Joan Festival.

PS I really surprised you with this one, didn't I? In due course you'll find out who left this for you...

"Majorca," Maria said slowly. "I've heard of Deià—it's an artists' colony in the Tramuntana mountains. Robert Graves lived there."

"A fourth journey," Rosie said, her voice barely above a whisper. "A fourth photograph."

They looked at each other, the realisation dawning simultaneously: Lisa had saved the most important revelation for last.

EPILOGUE

It was late June when they boarded their flight to Majorca, each woman carrying with her own thoughts and questions as they boarded the plane. Who was the woman in the photograph with Lisa, and why had she kept her existence a secret? What connection did this Spanish village have to the politically-engaged, cosmopolitan writer they had known? And what revelations awaited them that were so significant but could only be reveled after their lovely friend's death?

The answers lay across the sea, in a whitewashed village clinging to a Majorcan hillside. A village where Lisa Mack—or Elisabeta Montero—had begun her life's journey. A place that held secrets dark enough to drive her to erase her past, yet precious enough that she wanted a part of herself to return there after death.

Maria settled into her seat, clutching the blue leather book securely in her bag. She gazed out the window as the plane taxied toward the runway, watching England fall away beneath them. She thought of the three journeys they had already completed.

Little did they know that the mysteries of Deià would test

not only their understanding of their departed friend but the very bonds of their friendship. For in that sun-drenched village, shadows lurked—shadows of civil war, of family secrets, of betrayals and sacrifices—that would draw them into a story more complex and dangerous than any they could have imagined.

The final journey was just beginning, and nothing would ever be the same again.

ENDS...

THEY ARE OFF TO MAJORCA!

Follow our three intrepid heroines as they hit the party island in the Mediterranean. You can download the next instalment of the Sassy & Sixty adventures here:

UK:
My Book
US:
My Book

Printed in Great Britain
by Amazon